RESURRECT

A Whitney Steel Novel - Book 3

Kim Cresswell

KC Publishing

Resurrect/Kim Cresswell - 1st Edition
ISBN 978-0-9950578-2-1

Cover design by KC Book Cover Design

Subscribe to Kim's Quarterly Newsletter and keep up-to-date on exclusive content, upcoming releases, first-to-see book covers, contests, and more at www.kimcresswell.ca.

For Justin, Carla, Porter, and Peyton

In memory of Mary Beech
Death leaves a heartache no one can heal, love leaves a
memory no one can steal. — From a headstone in Ireland

ABOUT THE AUTHOR

Kim Cresswell resides in Ontario, Canada and is the award-winning author of the action-packed WHITNEY STEEL series.

Her debut romantic thriller, *Reflection* (A Whitney Steel Novel - Book One) has won numerous awards: RomCon®'s 2014 Readers' Crown Finalist (Romantic Suspense), InD'tale Magazine 2014 Rone Award Finalist (Suspense/Thriller), UP Authors Fiction Challenge Winner, Silicon Valley's Romance Writers of America (RWA) "Gotcha!" Romantic Suspense Winner, and an Honorable Mention in Calgary's (RWA) The Writer's Voice Contest.

Kim signed a 3-book German translation deal with Luzifer Verlagfor the first three books in the Whitney Steel series: *Reflection*, *Retribution,* and *Resurrect*. The popular series will be published in German beginning in 2019.

The Assassin Chronicles TV series, based on Kim's 4-book paranormal/supernatural thriller series: *Deadly Shadow (May 2018)*, *Invisible Truth, Assassin's Prophecy*, and *Vision of Fire* was in development with Council Tree Productions.

Web Site: www.kimcresswell.ca

Facebook: www.facebook.com/KimCresswellBooks

Twitter: http://twitter.com/kimcresswell

ALSO BY KIM CRESSWELL

The Whitney Steel Series
Reflection (Book One)
Retribution (Book Two)
Resurrect (Book Three)

The Assassin Chronicles Series
Deadly Shadow (Book One)

The Sum of all Tears Series
Icehaven (Book One)
Liberty (Book Two)

The Raina Storm Thriller Novella Series
Dawn of the Storm (Book One)
Dawn of the Enemy (Book Two)

Single Title Novellas
Lethal Journey

The True Crime Quickie Short Story Series
Real Life Evil
Murder on Sunset Strip
Garden of Bones
Edge of Madness

Chameleon
Backwoods Murder

**True Crime Anthologies Published
by Grinning Man Press**
Serial Killer Quarterly "21st Century Psychos"
Serial Killer Quarterly "Partners in Pain"
Serial Killer Quarterly "Unsolved in North America"
Serial Killer Quarterly "Cruel Britannia"
Serial Killer Quarterly "They Almost Got Away"
Serial Killer Quarterly "Lostmord: Murder in German"

CHAPTER ONE

D r. Matthew Fielding estimated he had six days to live.

He doubted he'd make it that long. Not judging by the harsh glint in the dark eyes staring at him through the clear visor. Inside the barren warehouse, the man wore a blue positive-pressure suit with its own air supply and clutched a gun awkwardly in his rubber-gloved hand. The spaceman-like suit would protect the man. For Fielding, on the other hand, it was already too late. Sweat trickled down the sides of his face, and his body trembled.

It had begun.

The high fever and chills were only the beginning. Soon, he'd experience the worst headache of his life, muscle and abdominal pain, nausea, and vomiting. Already, his internal organs burned as if set on fire, the pain insufferable. An hour ago, he'd noted a purplish-red maculopapular rash on his chest and shoulders, followed by a five-minute nosebleed.

"Do you have it?"

Fielding coughed, then nodded. "They're going to know the sample is missing."

"I'm planning on it." The man pointed the gun at a gray chest on a metal table against the brick wall. "Put the vial in there."

Fielding lifted his shaking hand and pulled out a glass tube from his shirt pocket. He walked across the room, his legs weak and wobbly, and pressed the red button on the portable refrigeration unit.

The lid hissed open, and he placed the tube inside. He eyed a second sample already in the unit. Worry worked through his body. "What do you plan on doing with these? It's not as if I'll be around to find out. We both know that."

The man waved the gun. "Close the lid."

He did as ordered and heard the suction of the vacuum seal, confirming the component was secure. Whatever the man was planning, it wasn't good. He'd learned that two days ago, after he'd come home from work to find the man in his home, threatening to kill his wife and daughter if he didn't do exactly as instructed. He'd had no choice. He would sacrifice himself if it meant keeping his family safe.

"Thanks to you, a new chimera virus. Just think about how much you have helped us today."

It was much worse than he thought. The man had what he needed: two different micro-organisms containing the necessary genes to replicate and create a new pandemic. Nausea boiled in his gut, and the room spun. He seized the edge of the table to steady himself and closed his eyes until the dizziness subsided.

He had worked in Nevada at Flatiron Sargasso Laboratories for the past fifteen years, one of only two privately-owned CDC/USDA registered BSL-4 labs in the United States, researching some of the most dangerous pathogens in the world: Marburg, Ebola, dengue and yellow fevers.

Fielding knew what the man was up to. He just didn't know the target's identity. Nor did he know which terrorist group the man belonged to, whether foreign or domestic. Not that it mattered, because he wasn't walking out of the warehouse alive. He erupted into a coughing fit, his throat dry and raw. He yanked a crumpled handkerchief out of his pants pocket and wiped his mouth. Blood soaked the white cloth, indicating hemorrhaging had started. He noticed the two new large bruises on the outside of his hands and wrists caused by the bleeding under his skin. Fear paralyzed his limbs. If the man didn't kill him first, shock, delirium and kidney failure would put him in a coma, followed by an agonizing death. Either way, he was a goner.

The man simply stood and observed, probably knowing he was in pain and his health was declining rapidly.

Coppery sour blood filled his mouth. He swallowed slowly, careful not to choke. "What's...the other organism you're using for the virus?"

"Smallpox. We're calling the virus, Resurrect. Seems fitting, don't you think? It's been a while since the world has experienced a large smallpox outbreak."

All the breath whooshed out of his lungs. Dear God. Bad enough Fielding had accidentally infected himself with Marburg while hastily trying to smuggle the sample out of the lab. He had to admit the security measures in place were lax at best, even after 9/11. The thought of this man infecting unsuspecting innocent people made him glad he was going to die long before the guilt of what he'd been forced to do killed him.

As he watched two other men in suits enter the warehouse, regret plagued his conscience, and tears filled his eyes. Why hadn't he spent more time with his wife, Janet, and his eighteen-year-old daughter, Scarlet? All those long hours, working at the lab and writing the dozens of scientific papers filled with research that had consumed years of his life. A waste of time. Time he wasn't going to be able to make up for. He knew that now.

The two men glanced at him then lifted the unit containing the viruses and headed to the open warehouse door where a box van waited, engine idling. Gas-laden exhaust filled the warehouse. They trudged up the ramp and placed the unit on the floor in the back.

His blurry gaze shifted to the man with the gun, and he saw it. A spark of awareness the end was inevitable. He closed his eyes. *Please forgive me…*

A gunshot cracked. The thunderous boom echoed and vibrated throughout the warehouse a split second before the bullet shattered his forehead and bored into his brain.

CHAPTER TWO

Palm Beach, Aruba

Whitney reclined in the lounge chair and watched Angel paddle back and forth across the shallow end of the swimming pool. The seven-year-old dunked her head in and out of the water and giggled.

"Good news." Blake handed her a glass of white wine and took a seat next to her. "Alejandro Quintero is dead."

She sat up and lowered her sunglasses. "Are you sure?"

"Definitely. I just spoke with Hal Decker. It's over. As of a week ago, he's no longer a threat. With Quintero and Pablo Sanchez out of the picture, I'm confident the *Sur del Calle* cartel will leave us alone. They have no reason to act on the Pablo's or Alejandro's personal vendettas. We're safe now."

"What happened?"

"Apparently, Chambers sent Hal and Angela Donahue on a covert mission to Colombia after the terrorist attack at the Diablo Canyon Nuclear Plant."

She remembered the day well, the images, the horror, and the tears. November 17th was the day Umar Sarouk, a radicalized American with the help of an al Qaeda terrorist cell in Yemen had committed the worst terrorist attack on US soil since 9/11. Thousands of Californians had been killed in the initial blast and thousands more were sick and dying from radiation poisoning. The state was still feeling the aftereffects of the fallout that had covered a fifty-mile radius surrounding the nuclear facility, changing the west coast for decades to come.

Since the attack, nuclear disaster preparedness exercises were done regularly at Nellis Air Force Base alongside the Nuclear Regulatory Commission, FEMA, state nuclear power plant operators, local and state officials, and hundreds of first responders.

"Their goal was to stop a second attack. I can't get into the details but in the end, the mission was a success. Alejandro was killed."

Alejandro's words drummed through her mind. *"You're like your father. You look just like him."* What he had said when she'd been kidnapped by Pablo continued to plague her to this day. Her father, an award-winning journalist, had died while on assignment in Colombia in 1997. She'd asked Blake to have his contacts poke around and see if they could find out more about her father's death, but nothing had come out of it. Her father had died in Colombia, exactly what she had been told.

"My God. I wasn't aware there was a second threat."

"This is first I've heard about it too."

She stared at him for a moment. "You aren't going to tell me how Alejandro was killed, are you?"

"Nope."

She understood sometimes he couldn't tell her specific details about certain off-the-books missions. It had been like that since they first met while he was working undercover for the FBI at ShawBioGen, pretending to be a security specialist to Nathan Shaw trying to learn more about his sister's death. Whitney knew many of those secrets still weighed heavily on him by the many sleepless nights.

"I can't wait to leave." She lowered her sunglasses and smiled. "Sofia will be thrilled to start college. It's been difficult for her being so isolated after losing her father. I'm also sure Angel will be elated to see her friends at school."

"It's been hard on all of us. I know my parents will be happy to have us back. I think I'm going to miss this living off the grid thing." Blake kissed her cheek then took a drink of his beer. "Six months in paradise with you, Angel and Sofia away from work does have its advantages. I haven't felt this relaxed in years—if ever."

It was heaven here. Beautiful, peaceful and a wonderful break from life. It would have been even better under different circumstances.

They had rented a three-bedroom villa on Palm Beach minutes from the turquoise crystal-clear water and powdery white sands of the southern Caribbean Sea, about six kilometers from the capital city of Oranjestad. They'd barely had time to catch their breath after fleeing Las Vegas for their own safety following their August wedding. She'd love to return one day and have a real honeymoon but right now all she wanted was to go home, get back to work, and to have some normalcy for Angel and Sofia's sake. They had both been through so much.

She exhaled a long sigh of relief knowing Alejandro was dead and that Nathan Shaw was in prison waiting to be executed. They could finally get back to their lives.

✳ ✳ ✳

Three days later...

In SecuraCorp's conference room, Whitney sat and stared at District Attorney Jason Kurtz, her eyes wide with disbelief. She wasn't sure she'd heard the DA correctly. "Nathan Shaw is out on twenty million dollars bail? Did I hear that right?"

The room went quiet and his eyes held a serious look. "Unfortunately, you did. I know it's hard to believe. The retrial is scheduled in six months. In the meantime, he's under house arrest complete with an ankle monitor. The Department of Corrections will be monitoring him closely. He is not allowed to leave his home unless it's for a medical appointment. Every appointment requires approval according to Judge Minton's orders unless it's an emergency."

A chill drove down her spine and panic built inside her chest. *Six months. This had to be a bad dream.*

"As long as that bastard is alive, he's dangerous." Blake's jaw tightened. "You of all people know that, Jason. Not only do we have Angel to protect, we also have Sofia."

"I know." The district attorney's brows furrowed. "His lawyer was able to convince the Nevada Supreme Court that he wasn't provided with adequate representation. I've only seen it happen once before."

Blake's eyes narrowed and a vein in his neck pulsated. "We all know Shaw masterminded the whole thing, right down to pretending his lawyer had mistakenly hired a retired civil engineer to testify about the gun evidence at his trial. How much did he pay that scumbag, Warren Demotteo?"

"So far there isn't any evidence of any payment. Demotteo's bank records are squeaky clean."

Whitney heard the concern in the DA's voice and that made her worry even more. "That's not surprising. Nathan would pay cash to cover himself. The man would never leave a trail. He never has in the past."

Jason nodded in agreement. "If we can dig something up on him maybe we can get him back in prison where he belongs. I can't say I've ever had a case go south like this one especially when the accused was sentenced to death. I'm just as shocked as you are the judge allowed bail after everything Shaw has done. I'm sorry. I know this isn't the news you want to hear. You just got rid of one problem and now this."

It certainly wasn't news she wanted or needed to hear. Just when she thought the man would finally be out of their lives, Nathan was back, resurrected from death row.

It was bad enough they had been forced to go into hiding. They'd only been home for a few days and now this. Whitney wondered if they would ever be free of Nathan Shaw.

Blake shoved his hands into his jean's pockets. "He probably paid off the judge. Nothing would surprise me or the lengths he will go to. He's already proved that by hiring a hit man to kill my sister, had Senator Mason Bailey killed in front of Whitney, murdered District Attorney Kate Letham, and hired a nutcase who murdered George Raines in an explosion meant to kill Whitney. And let's not forget he tried to kill me too and had a hand in helping Pablo Sanchez kidnap Whitney." The tone of his voice turned hard and louder. "Those aren't things I can just push aside and get over. Too many people we cared about are dead because of him."

"You don't need to remind me, Blake. Believe me, I do

understand. The State of Nevada wants him out of the picture too. We'll keep digging and see what we can find. Everyone in my office is working around the clock."

The DA's tone sounded genuine. "We do appreciate what you're doing, Jason." Let's just hope it's enough, Whitney wanted to add but decided not to.

"I need to get going." The DA stood and snatched up his black leather briefcase from the floor. "I've got to be in court in an hour. I'll be in touch."

After Jason left, Whitney remained silent and stared out the window trying to understand how a man who had killed so many people was free on bail. She felt Blake's hand on her shoulder.

"Bet you wish we were back in Aruba. I know I do."

They could finally get back to their lives…

She stood and smoothed her skirt still trying to grasp the bad news. "I'm really worried."

"Me too. I'll speak with my parents and see if they can help with Angel after school. I'll also have someone keep an eye on Sofia until Shaw is back behind bars. I think it would devastate her if we pulled her out of college at this point."

"It would. I want to make sure they are both protected at all times." A shudder drove through her body. "What if Nathan decides to leak the truth about Angel? Imagine the media circus if the public learned she is an identical copy of your sister, Claire."

"I don't think he would release the information because it would prove he's guilty. It would be out of character. He's never admitted to anything, ever."

Out of character or not, there still was a chance. "I'm also concerned about Sofia. She's been through enough dealing with the loss of her father. She misses her mother too. I know even with Alejandro dead it's probably still not safe for her to visit her mother. Maybe one day."

Lines etched his forehead. He became quiet and Whitney knew he was thinking about Oscar. Not only had Sofia lost her father, Blake had lost his good friend in Colombia while trying to rescue Whitney from the cartel.

"I promise you we'll figure this out." Blake laced his fingers through hers and kissed her forehead. "For now, let's try to get on with our lives the best we can and hopefully Jason can come up with a way to get Shaw back in prison sooner than later. Everything will be okay."

His reassurance did nothing to ease her jitters. Right now, she needed to be busy and focus on something else. "I think I'm going to stop by the station and try to get in a few hours of work. Travis has been bugging me about following up on a story, something about a local scientist found dead."

Blake kissed her neck. "Your boss, Travis Wade, is a slave driver. You know we could just go home and call it a day. A little hard to focus on work now especially with that bad news."

Tiny shivers danced along her neck the moment his lips touched her skin. Whitney wanted to forget today had happened. But she couldn't. "I'd love to but I have work to do and so do you. I saw how impatient Michelle looked when we came in. I'm betting your secretary has months worth of work for you."

"Yeah, you're probably right." He opened the door.

His secretary was on the other side with tears in her eyes.

Whitney touched the woman's arm. "What's wrong, Michelle?"

The young woman hesitated for a moment. "I just got

a phone call from the police. My Uncle Mathew—is dead."

"Come sit down." Blake guided her by the arm into the conference room.

Whitney took a seat next to Michelle at the table and passed her a box of tissues. Her heart squeezed at the sight of the woman's pain. Whitney had been there many times. Mason...George...her father... "I'm so sorry. What happened?

"I don't know. I asked the detective and he said he wasn't able to tell me anything other than he's dead." Michelle plucked a handful of tissues from the box and wiped her eyes and nose.

"Do you remember the detective's name?"

Michelle sniffled. "I think his name was Tony White. Something like that. The conversation is a blur."

"I'll go and see what I can find out," Blake said.

Whitney nodded and patted Michelle's hand. "I really am sorry for your loss. What can I do?"

"I just want to know what happened." Tears spilled down the woman's cheeks. "My uncle—he's a scientist. Maybe something happened to him at the lab. Or a car accident or something. I need to know."

This was the story her boss wanted her to follow up on. Whitney tried not to show any reaction and looked away for a second. Uneasiness spiked in her veins. With Nathan Shaw released on bail and Michelle's uncle dead, she couldn't help but wonder if the two events were connected. It wasn't as if Nathan hadn't had a scientist killed before; Blake's sister and Carmen Lacey who both worked at ShawBioGen. She prayed she was wrong. "How about we wait and see what Blake can find out, okay? I'll get you some water. I'll be right back."

Whitney rushed down the hallway and into Blake's

office. He was on the phone.

"It's okay." He held up the receiver and covered the mouthpiece with his hand. "I'm on hold. How's she doing?"

"Not good at all. She's devastated." She paused for a moment and her hands started to tremble. "Blake, her uncle is the dead scientist that Travis wanted me to follow up on."

"Jesus." Worry lines crept across his forehead.

He slowly put down the phone and she knew what he was thinking.

"Please tell me her uncle's death isn't somehow related to Shaw?"

After everything they had been through with Nathan Shaw, Whitney was dumbfounded at the thought. "I don't know what to think. Maybe it's just a coincidence but I have a feeling we're going to find out."

✳ ✳ ✳

Blake had noticed the panic in Whitney's eyes when they had learned Nathan Shaw was out on bail.

He leaned back in his chair and cracked his knuckles. He'd felt sucker-punched in the gut by the news. There was no way he was taking a wait and see approach this time around. He had a bad feeling about Michelle's uncle, a hollow queasiness in the pit of his stomach that wouldn't go away. The only so-called coincidences in their lives always involved Nathan Shaw. Blake wanted him dead and was willing to look after it personally, but he couldn't allow his personal feelings to get in the way. There was too much at stake. Too much to lose. Whitney, Angel, and Sofia. Not to mention, he didn't want to spend the rest of his life behind bars.

He forced the thought from his mind and made a quick phone call to his parents to have them pick up Angel after school. The only thing that was important was to make sure everyone he cared about was safe and remained that way.

His business partner, Mike Jacobs, rushed into the office dressed in a baggie white T-shirt and faded black jeans. He stopped in mid-stride. Concern raked across his face. "Christ, I heard the news. How can that asshole be out on bail?"

"Obviously, he paid off a lot of people including the judge. Exactly what he always does. But this time he isn't getting away with it. We're going to find a way to get him back in a cell. I'm not waiting for the DA to figure it out. Not this time."

Mike sat down in the chair across from him and leaned his elbows on the desk. "I don't blame you one bit. What do you want me to do?"

Even though both men had left the FBI immediately after Nathan Shaw had been arrested and started an investigation-security firm, off the record, they were still called upon by the Bureau for certain discreet operations. The last mission had sent them to Colombia after Pablo Sanchez had kidnapped Whitney. He had already called Trent Chambers, his former SAC, to give him the heads up.

"I spoke with Chambers and he said we could use whatever resources we need. I need two things." He checked his watch. Ten-thirty. "Give Paul McBride a call and have him keep an eye on Sofia and make sure she's protected at all times. Tell him to stay in the shadows until I have a chance to talk to her later today. I don't want to scare her." Blake grabbed a pen and wrote the college's address on a piece of paper and passed it to Mike.

"You got it."

"Second. Get in touch with Joe Cally." He scribbled another address down and handed it across the desk. "Kurtz said Shaw rented a house in Henderson instead of staying on-site at ShawBioGen. I'm not sure why, but have Cally watch the place and let me know if Shaw has any visitors. Make sure he gets video or photos. Anything. I don't want to miss a single thing."

Mike nodded and took the paper. "Looks like Shaw's hanging out in the ritzy part of town. I still can't believe he's out."

Whitney poked her head inside the door and frowned when she saw Mike. "You didn't get much of a day off after looking after the business for months."

"That's okay. This is more important. The thought of that asshole free out on bail makes me sick."

"You and me both." She locked eyes with Blake. "I'm going to head to the station now. I sent Michelle home and called the temp service to replace her for a few days. Someone will be here within the next few hours."

He smiled, grateful she was in his life. She looked strikingly beautiful in a tight black skirt and white top with her brown hair cascading a few inches past her shoulders. Her green eyes still held a hint of panic, or maybe it was an awareness their lives had suddenly changed once again.

"Thanks. I'll catch up with you in a few hours. Be careful. Let me know what you find out about Michelle's uncle. I'm still waiting for a call back from Tony White."

"I will—especially now." She swung her purse strap over her shoulder. "Mike, please keep him out of trouble."

"Always."

After Whitney left, Mike had a confused expression on his face.

"What's going on with Michelle? Did I miss something?"

"She got a call about her uncle. He's dead. She's pretty busted up about it." Blake leaned back in the chair and put his hands behind his head. "I left a message for the detective who'd called her. The guy works homicide. I wasn't about to tell Michelle that. She would have freaked out. She was upset enough about her uncle." He paused for a moment. "You're going to love this, though. Her uncle was a scientist."

Mike's eyes widened. "Sounds a little too familiar to me. I'm not liking this at all. Not after everything that's happened and not today with Shaw free."

"Exactly what I was thinking." Blake thought about his sister, Claire, a molecular biologist who had worked for Shaw. She was dead because of the man. He cursed under his breath. "The timing stinks. Nathan Shaw is free. Another scientist is dead. What are the chances?"

CHAPTER THREE

I n her seventh-floor office at News3, Whitney glanced out the window at the giant 3d-looking clouds floating by then back to her laptop screen. From what she had learned about Dr. Matthew Fielding was minimal at best. He had worked at Flatiron Sargasso Laboratories for the past fifteen years and had published a dozen papers about deadly pathogens for some of the most prestigious science and medical journals in the country. From the little information she could find, it appeared the man was well-respected by his colleagues for his work. She'd also discovered he had a wife and teenage daughter and that made her sad. She remembered the look on Sofia's face the moment she knew her father was dead at the safe house in Colombia.

Jerry Maxwell, her cameraman, sat on the black leather sofa flipping through the pages of a magazine. "Wade said he'd have security for us in about ten minutes."

Whitney felt some relief knowing they weren't going out on assignment without security, not after what had happened the last time. She tried not to think about how Pablo Sanchez's men had kidnapped her in the courthouse parking lot during Nathan Shaw's sentencing and had taken her to Colombia, or how Jerry had been shot in the leg.

The sane voice in her head ordered her to stay still. Even though she had a black belt in karate and was skilled at crushing a person's windpipe or disarming a knife-wielding attacker, she wasn't stupid enough to take on three guys that were double her height and weight with guns aimed at her. All she could do was watch, stay as calm as possible, and hope someone would see what was going on and call the police.

When Jerry had the live feed setup, he stood in front of them, camera ready. His voice trembled. "You're on."

The third man, the tallest of the group, pulled a red and white bandana out of a small plastic bag he had stuffed in the pocket of his jeans.

He pressed the moist cloth over her mouth and nose and held it there.

She squirmed and kicked but it was useless. Her head started to buzz. The sickly-sweet smell mixed with the rotten odor of strong cleaning solution invaded her head...

She pushed the other horrible memories away of the men she was forced to kill to save her own life, the images vivid in her mind as if it had happened yesterday.

Everything is going to be okay. Breathe.

She stared at the photograph online of the scientist determined to focus and shove the past back where it belonged.

Matthew Fielding didn't look anything like Whitney had imagined. He was an attractive man in his fifties with smiling dark green eyes and perfectly styled light brown hair parted to one side. He certainly wasn't the academic-looking type she'd imagined. He looked more like a rugged athlete. "It's odd there isn't much information about Fielding. For a man who was quite celebrated for his work, it's as if he barely existed. I contacted my source at the Las Vegas Police Department and she couldn't tell me anything about how the man died. She was able to get a copy of the police report. Most of it has been mysteriously redacted. I've never seen anything like this before." Whitney passed the report to him.

He looked at the paper and raised a bushy eyebrow. "That doesn't make sense."

Jerry was right. It didn't make sense. Someone was covering up something. Who? Why?

"When I asked her why it was redacted she said she had no idea."

"At least they didn't black out the address where the scientist's body was discovered. Do you want to start there?"

She nodded. "As soon as our security shows up." Uneasiness welled up inside her and moisture broke out on her forehead at the thought of working on a story again after the last one almost got her killed. "Are you nervous? This is the first time for both of us since that day at the courthouse."

He stood, tossing the magazine on the coffee table. "A bit. It's not a day I want to remember."

Neither did Whitney.

She was even more on edge after hearing about Nathan Shaw. She had assumed, and expected, the man was going to stay behind bars until he was executed. Boy, was she wrong.

The brass drone of her boss' voice startled her. She looked up to see Travis standing in the doorway sporting a loose-fitting light blue dress shirt and jeans. The outfit was far from his usual attire of black dress pants and white shirt. Travis Wade was about the same age as Whitney, in his late-thirties with thinning brown hair, a beak-long nose and was nothing like the arrogant jerk-of-a-boss Mike Wildell at WBNN that she used to work for in Florida. Travis didn't care what she did as long as she got the story before any of the other news outlets. It was what she was the best at. Exactly why he had hired her.

"Your husband sent over a guy named, Mike, to keep an eye on you two. He's waiting in the parking lot."

Even though SecuraCorp provided security for numerous television stations in Las Vegas and some of the largest casinos, Whitney wasn't expecting Blake to send Mike. They were in good hands and for that, she loved her husband even more. Blake continued to make her feel safe after the kidnapping. It wasn't as if she couldn't look after herself. She had a third-degree black belt in karate and had extensive weapons training yet even with her skills, she still hadn't been able to stop Pablo Sanchez from kidnapping her and whisking her off to Colombia. She also was confident Angel and Sofia were safe. Blake wouldn't have it any other way.

She closed the laptop. "Thanks, Travis. I'll let you know what I find out. Will you be here?"

He checked his watch. "For about another hour, and then I have a meeting with the station's brass." He glanced over his shoulder as he walked toward the door. "Text if you need me."

She turned to Jerry, her nerves tight as piano strings. "Ready?"

He nodded. "The van is loaded. Let's roll."

* * *

"The transfer of the samples to the lab is complete," the man said, as he lit a cigarette and watched his fingers tremble slightly. He clutched his cell phone tighter.

He was still concerned after dealing with Fielding at the warehouse even though he had worn a protective spacesuit. He knew what he'd agreed to do was going to be tough emotionally, always wondering if he could have possibly been infected like the scientist. He was re-assured the protective rubber of the suit along with the separate air supply had kept him safe making it impossible to become infected. He was only doing this for the payday, a big one. Retirement was expensive. His friend on the other hand, well, he had his own reasons.

"Good. We should be ready within thirty-six to seventy-two hours."

"Our mutual friend will be happy. Very happy."

The man agreed. "Our flight is booked, and we'll be out of the Las Vegas just in time." He exhaled a large puff of smoke. He'd be glad when this was over. For his part, he'd already received the large payment in his off-shore account in St. Lucia. A few more days and he and his family would be on relaxing on the beach without a worry in the world.

"Have the men you hired to help transport the viruses been taken care of? We don't want any loose threads, as they say."

"They're no longer a problem. Everything has been looked after." He had done the imaginable. The men were gone, their bodies weighted down with cement blocks in the bottom of the Humboldt River. Not something he was proud of but a necessary move to ensure they never spoke a word about what went on at the warehouse. "Everything is in place. I'll be in contact."

❋ ❋ ❋

A half hour later, Jerry, slowed the satellite van and

rolled to a stop. "Looks like state troopers are ahead directing traffic. They have the area cordoned off. It looks like they're making drivers detour south onto Warbonnet Way." He inched the vehicle forward a few yards and stopped again waiting for the traffic to move.

Whitney leaned forward in the seat and stared out the windshield. Something wasn't right. "But we're still about three blocks away from where Fielding's body was found. What's up with the barricade?"

"I have no idea. It doesn't look like we're going to get near the warehouse."

An unmarked white van sped by in the opposite lane.

Whitney watched as the troopers lifted the wooden structure to one side and allowed the vehicle through. Instinct kicked in. One way or another she was getting this story. "There's a health food store on Warbonnet. We'll stop there. Are you up for a little hiking?" She checked the rear-view mirror and spotted Mike's cherry-red '69 Camaro two car-lengths behind them.

"Sure." The van lurched forward, and Jerry made a right turn onto the street. He drove a block and a half and steered into the lot of the health food store.

Mike pulled up and parked next to them. After shutting off the engine, he got out of the car. "What's going on?"

"Apparently, we're walking in." Jerry jumped out of the van and opened the back doors then grabbed his camera from the back and set it on the ground.

"It's a bad idea," Mike said.

Jerry shrugged. "Talk to the boss. Good luck changing her mind."

Mike walked to the other side of the van. "They've got it blocked off for a reason, Whitney."

"I just want to get closer and get a shot of the warehouse where Fielding's body was discovered. It's my job. You know that." She snatched her slip-on running shoes out of her shoulder bag and put them on, flinging her high-heels into the front seat of the van. She banged the door shut and squared her shoulders. "You're either coming with us or you aren't."

He shook his head. "You aren't giving me much of a choice."

"I know." She squinted in the sunlight and smiled at him grateful he was with them in case anything happened. At six-four and muscular Mike looked intimidating as hell to most people. Blake had known him for years after they met in the Marines and had worked together at the FBI before starting their security business. He was a good guy. Someone you could trust.

She slung the strap of her purse over her shoulder and started walking in the direction of the warehouse. Warm afternoon heat touched her skin and a light breeze ruffled her hair.

The area was made up of mostly commercial and industrial properties so they wouldn't have to sneak into home owner's backyards and risk getting caught or arrested but there still was a risk. A risk she was willing to take.

In the distance, she heard loud thumping, banging and clanking. The noise sounded like some type of construction going on. She spotted the top of a construction crane on the other side of the row of buildings.

Whitney stopped and brought up the GPS map on her cell phone. "That's the warehouse." She pointed to the six-storey red brick building next to a furniture manufacturing plant. Colorful graffiti and gang signs marred the back wall of the warehouse. On the second floor, most of the windows were gone, broken by vandals or weather or age.

Jerry wiped the sweat from his forehead with the back of his hand. "There's a pathway over there. We might be able to get a good shot of the front of the building from there."

Mike remained quiet and Whitney knew he didn't approve of what she was doing by the worry lines on his forehead.

As they headed down a long narrow alley like a canyon between the two buildings. A choking, nauseating stench of rotting garbage, chemicals and urine permeated the air when they walked past an overloaded trash bin.

Jerry shook his head and scrunched up his face. "Jesus. I wonder when the last time the thing was emptied?"

"By the looks of it probably not for months." Whitney picked up her pace determined to get away from the smell. The closer she got to the corner of the warehouse, the stronger the rush of anticipation and adrenaline mixed together.

An earth-shattering bang filled the air. Glass shattered and crunched. The ground below her feet vibrated. Whitney instinctively ducked.

"What the hell is going on?" Mike asked, as he cautiously walked to the edge of the building.

Whitney rushed behind him while Jerry hiked the camera up on his shoulder.

Mike stopped and crouched.

She peeked around the corner.

A thick cloud of dirt and dust curled to the sky and made it difficult to see. When the air finally cleared, she spotted the crane with a wrecking ball attached and a bulldozer.

She glanced at Mike, confused. "Why are they demolishing the building?"

"I have no idea but it's not safe. We need to leave before they hit this outside wall and it comes down on us."

Whitney glanced over her shoulder and yelled at Jerry. "Are you getting this?"

He gave her a thumbs-up and continued filming.

Whitney continued to watch.

A large contingency of police vehicles lined the perimeter of the parking lot and blocked the entrance to the warehouse. Two men with greasy long hair dressed in ragged torn jeans and T-shirts tripped out of one of the doors of the building, staggered, and collapsed to the ground on their hands and knees. Their skin looked white, almost ghost-like, their faces expressionless.

A large unmarked black box van sped into the parking lot and stopped about two-hundred yards from the bulldozer.

The hairs on the back of her neck stood up.

Four people dressed in full orange biosafety suits lumbered out of the van's back door, and Whitney knew she was on to something.

Mike grabbed her arm and yanked. "We need to get out of here. Now!"

CHAPTER FOUR

While Blake waited for the secretary from the temp service to arrive he was confident that everyone in his life was safe. He still had the same sinking feeling in his stomach that somehow Michelle's uncle's death was linked to Nathan Shaw. He didn't know how, but he was going to find out.

The office phone rang. By the third ring, he remembered Whitney had sent Michelle. He grabbed the receiver and answered the call hoping it was Tony White, so he could learn more about Michelle's uncle. "SecuraCorp."

"I heard that our lovely Miss Steel and you were married."

The low nasal tone of Nathan Shaw's voice droned in his ear and his pulse sped up. That didn't take long. Blake knew Shaw would call him just like he'd done in the past. He'd just hoped it was going to happen later rather than sooner.

"She looked stunning in her cream-colored wedding dress. Absolutely gorgeous."

His free hand curled into a fist. How the hell did he know about Whitney's wedding dress? His mind bounced in every direction trying to recount the faces of everyone at the wedding. Someone had fed Shaw the information. Anyone who had attended the wedding was either family, close friends, FBI agents he'd known for almost two decades, and four US marshals he trusted with his life. He needed a copy of the guest list.

"What do you want, Shaw?"

"To offer my congratulations, of course. I hope married life is treating you well." A long pause of silence. "However, I was thinking it would be nice to see the child. I'm sure she's grown a lot since those days at the lab. Does she look more like your sister each day?"

Angel? Blake's jaw went taut and he wanted to reach through the phone line and strangle the bastard. "You want to see the child you planned on killing? Not a chance in hell are you *ever* getting near her. It will never happen."

"That's really too bad. Imagine what the media will do when they learn the child is the world's first cloned human—that I created her in my lab at ShawBioGen and you and your beautiful bride adopted her, knowing that information. Do you really want that type of chaos in your life? Your honeymoon would be over quite quickly, I would say. Remember, Barnett. I really have nothing to lose by contacting the media. I have nothing to lose, period. I've told you before. You aren't going to win against me."

"I'm sick of your threats, Shaw. I've had enough of you being in our lives. Call me again, or Whitney, and I will make certain there's a truck-load of chaos in your life. I'll kill you myself." At least with Shaw out of prison, he could say exactly what he wanted to without being recorded.

"I see you still don't have that temper of yours under —"

"Fuck off." Blake smashed the receiver down, knocking over the phone.

He was sick and tired of the man constantly taunting him. Now he had a bigger problem to deal with. If Shaw made good on his threat to contact the media about Angel they'd never have any peace and quiet and it would also make it more difficult for him to protect everyone. There was no way he was allowing the man to see Angel. Shaw had pointed a gun at her head prepared to kill her to keep his illegal cloning project a secret from the world. Worry wore at his gut. He couldn't tell Whitney. Not yet. She'd be devastated by the news.

The office phone rang again and his muscles flinched. He grabbed the phone hoping it wasn't Shaw. "Secura-Corp."

"Hey, Blake. I got your message."

He recognized Tony White's gravelly voice on the other. "Thanks for getting back to me."

"No problem. There isn't much I can tell you about Mathew Fielding other than he worked at Flatiron Sargasso Laboratories. Dispatch got a 0-54, a possible dead body. An anonymous caller phoned it in and said some guy looked dead. I got a call to go to a warehouse on West Sunset Road. When I arrived, blockades were set up three blocks in every direction and the police chief told me I wasn't needed—to go home. It was a weird scene. It didn't look like anyone was going in or out of the perimeter."

"Any idea on what might have happened? How Fielding died?"

"None. Everything is hush-hush. Something big went down but no one is talking not about it. Not even the chief."

"If you hear anything can you let me know? It would at least give Michelle some closure if she knew something about her uncle's death."

"Sure, I'll be in touch. Oh, congrats on getting married. Better you than me. I've been down that path far too many times."

Blake grinned, knowing the man had been divorced three times. It wasn't an easy life being married to a homicide cop. "Thanks, Tony."

He ended the call and leaned back in the chair. He had to admit what Tony had said about the warehouse was odd. The local cops usually didn't usually barricade off three blocks in each direction. His friend was right. Something was off.

After working for the FBI for fifteen years, Blake knew anything was possible. He'd seen it all. Nathan Shaw was the perfect example. Who would have thought a multi-billionaire philanthropist had been working on an illegal human cloning project for years in the Nevada desert and no one had known about it? Blake would never have known if Claire hadn't turned up dead. Her death had been originally ruled an accident. He knew it wasn't true. His sister would never have gotten onto a boat when she was terrified of water and didn't know how to swim. Shaw had given the order because she knew too much and was about to expose the truth about his cloning project. She was lured onto a boat and the killer had blocked the exhaust outlets allowing carbon monoxide to accumulate inside the cabin and poison her. At least she hadn't suffered.

He still couldn't shake the feeling that Nathan was involved with the scientist. His gut was never wrong. There had to be a connection. He flipped open his laptop and began searching through his old files.

After his temporary secretary, Rachel Marks, was settled in at her desk in the reception area, Blake continued to read document after document about Shaw's past. Much of the information he'd gathered while working undercover for the Bureau. Then he found something.

Shaw had donated fifteen-million-dollars to Flatiron Sargasso Laboratories, a privately-owned CDC/USDA registered BSL-4 lab. What he discovered wasn't a smoking gun. Far from it. Only a causal link between Shaw and Fielding. It wasn't unusual for the man to donate large amounts of cash to charities or other causes. On the other hand, anything with Shaw's name attached to it was suspicious.

He did a quick Internet search for Flatiron Sargasso and learned the lab dealt with some of the most dangerous and exotic agents, mainly pathogens that posed a high individual risk of aerosol-transmitted infections, and life-threatening diseases that were fatal where there were no vaccines or treatments.

Blake rubbed his chin. Why would Nathan donate a large sum of money to a BSL-4 lab when he owned his own lab, ShawBioGen? He didn't like where his thoughts were heading. He grabbed his cell phone and dialed Mike's number. After the fourth ring, he finally answered.

"Yeah."

It sounded as if Mike was out of breath. "Where are you?"

"With Whitney and Jerry. We were just at the warehouse where Michelle's uncle died. They were starting to demolish the building. Get this. There were four guys in biosafety suits. This isn't good, Blake."

His eyes roamed to his laptop screen.

Life-threatening diseases that were fatal where there were no vaccines or treatments.

Shit. "Did any of you go inside the warehouse?"

"No. The area is locked down."

He breathed a silent sigh. "Get the hell away from that place. Far away. We don't know what we're dealing with. I just found something that links Nathan Shaw to the scientist."

❊ ❊ ❊

After Mike, Jerry and Whitney returned to Secura-Corp, Whitney was still trying to digest what she'd witnessed at the warehouse. As Blake watched the video Jerry had taken, she couldn't get the image of the two men who had collapsed out of her head. It was clear the men were very sick. It was also clear the people dressed in the orange biosafety suits were from the CDC's Rapid Response Team.

Years back, she had done a story about the Centers for Disease Control and Prevention about the Lyme Disease epidemic in the United States and had interviewed one of their 'disease detectives' as well as Director Don Greeden. The CDC had ignored the severity of the epidemic while tens of thousands of people continued to be sick with little or no treatment. Sadly, nothing much had changed even with her award-winning investigative report. The CDC continued to deny the epidemic while playing up other less serious illnesses that only affected a very small number of people, helping to make millions for some of the biggest pharmaceutical companies in the country. It was a sad situation, and Whitney didn't trust the CDC one bit. What were they hiding this time?

When Jerry finished playing the video, Blake cracked

his knuckles and remained quiet.

For some reason, he didn't appear shocked by Jerry's footage and Whitney wasn't sure why.

"It gets worse. Nathan Shaw is connected to the lab where Fielding worked."

Her breath caught in her throat and for a second, she was speechless. "You have got to be kidding."

"I wish I was. A fifteen-million-dollar connection. He made the donation six months ago. Clearly, the transaction was looked after by his lawyer." Blake handed her a piece of paper.

She read the information and her stomach sank. "While he was in prison? This is unbelievable."

"So, you were right. Shaw has his greasy fingers in the pot. We just don't know how deep, other than he donated to Fielding's lab. This can't be a coincidence especially when the transaction was made while he was behind bars." Mike rubbed the back of his neck and continued. "Why risk being involved? I mean, as stupid as it sounds, there is a small chance he could be acquitted during the retrial. It's not likely but stranger things have happened."

She saw the anger in Blake's eyes the way they narrowed. She felt the same way. Angry that the man one way or another continued to be in their lives. "He had better not be acquitted. Not after what he's done." She thought about Mason and George and how they were both killed. Whitney pushed the memories from her mind not wanting to relive the pain. "He's not going to get away with this. We need to find more to tie him to Dr. Fielding."

Jerry stuffed his hands in his pockets. "We still don't know what went down with Fielding or how he died."

Her mind drifted to the police report. "I got a hold

of the police report but most of it was mysteriously redacted."

Mike's eyebrows rose. "Information was blacked out?"

"Yes."

Blake shook his head. "That alone makes no sense. I'll contact Chambers and see what he can find out on his end. Someone is trying to cover up something. We just don't exactly know what."

"And what the hell was going on at the warehouse? Why the sudden demolition?" Jerry asked. "Getting a permit doesn't work that quickly. It can take months, sometimes years. Not a couple of days."

"Just more evidence that someone is trying to whitewash what went down."

Whitney touched his arm. "How did the CDC know where to find Fielding's body?"

"Tony White said an anonymous caller phoned it in and said there was a guy who looked dead in the warehouse."

His secretary popped her head in the doorway. "Sorry to interrupt. Hmm…a Joe Cally is on line two."

"Thanks." Blake scooped up the receiver and pressed the blinking line two button.

Whitney watched the older woman leave. She hoped Michelle was doing okay at home. It wasn't easy losing someone you cared about. More than anything Whitney wished she had the answers Michelle needed about her uncle's death. She didn't. At least not yet.

"Hey man—Demotteo? When? Is he alone?" A long pause of silence before Blake spoke again. He looked at Whitney, and then to Mike. "Okay. Keep me posted." He hung up the phone and looked up at Whitney. "That slimy lawyer, Warren Demotteo, showed up at Shaw's house. Cally said the man's been there for the past hour."

"They're probably working on a plan for the upcoming trial." She wanted to be sick the moment she said the words.

"Yeah, and collaborating on who's next on the list to be paid off," Mike added.

"That wouldn't surprise me one bit."

She wondered how much Nathan's lawyer knew? Had Nathan confessed anything to the man? Whitney doubted it. It wasn't in the man's nature. He'd never taken responsibility for anything he'd done in the past.

Blake glanced up at the wall clock. "We still have a few hours before my parent's pick up Angel at school. I'm going to slip out and talk to Chambers and see what I can find out. After I'll speak with Kurtz about Nathan's wonderfully supportive donation. I'm sure he'll be thrilled even though it's not enough to nail the bastard."

She noted the aggravated tone of his voice and his clutched fists. "I think Jerry and I are going to make a trip to Flatiron Sargasso Laboratories and see what we can find out about what Dr. Fielding was working on."

"Good idea. Mike, you stay with Whitney and Jerry. No one is to take any chances especially when we have no idea what we're dealing with." Blake paused for a moment and turned to both men. "I want to talk to Whitney alone for a moment."

"Sure. I'll be out in the parking lot." Mike bounced out of the chair and walked to the door while Jerry grabbed his camera from the floor.

After the two men left, Whitney had a bad feeling deep in her stomach. "What is it?"

"It's not good. You need to know this before you leave." He opened his laptop and spun it around so she could see the screen.

As she read, her heart rate increased. All it took was the words, "dangerous agents and life-threatening diseases...blood starts to seep from the skin, mouth, eyes, and ears...internal organs hemorrhage." She had to stop reading. "Dear God. The two men at the warehouse. They were infected with something—with one of those diseases."

"It appears that way. We both know the CDC were there. The scientist had something, and whatever he had probably killed him and will end up killing those other men. If they aren't dead already."

Her thoughts turned to Angel and Sofia. They should have all stayed in Aruba where they were safe. They should never have come home.

As if reading her mind, he grabbed her hand and held it. "They're safe. Try not to worry."

"How can I not worry? We've only been home for a couple of days and we've learned Nathan Shaw is out of prison and Michelle's uncle was infected with something that more than likely killed him."

Blake stood and wrapped his arms around her and held her tight. "Sofia and Angel are safe. Cally and McBride would never let anything happen to them. I trust them with my life and theirs."

She rested her head on his shoulder and felt safe in his arms but that refuge rapidly dissipated. "Maybe we should just leave again until all this settles down."

"That's not like you. There's a huge story here. You've never walked away from a story. George would never let you walk away. Neither will I."

She couldn't help but smile when Blake mentioned George's name. Whitney could almost hear George's voice in her head. *What happened to the Woman of Steel? She would never have passed up a story.* She missed him more than ever, missed that father figure in her life just as much as she missed her own father.

"I've never had two girls to worry about and you. Things are different now." One question plagued her mind like a constant itch she couldn't reach. "If an anonymous caller reported Fielding's body then couldn't the caller be infected too?"

❋ ❋ ❋

Whitney slipped on her sunglasses to lessen the glare of the late-afternoon sunlight. After Jerry parked the van, she stared at the sprawling four-storey glass and brick structure.

Flatiron Sargasso Laboratories was a modern looking building with a barely noticeable silver logo on the double front doors. The structure could easily fit into a suburban office area where no one would give it a second glance. It wasn't elaborate like Nathan's ShawBioGen with its metal "S" towering over the entrance, picturesque gardens, and on-site employee housing.

Blake was right. There was a story here. Whitney could feel it. A shiver spiked down her back. She had to admit she was a bit nervous about the type pathogens the lab dealt with. She'd already made an appointment to speak with Dell Summers, the facility's Director of Science. She needed to learn more about Matthew Fielding and what he was working on before he died. She'd also needed to choose her questions wisely otherwise the interview would be shut down in a matter of seconds.

She turned to Jerry. "You'll have to wait here since no cameras are allowed inside."

"I figured that much. BSL-4 labs don't like giving tours unless it's a newly built facility and before it's considered hot when the lethal bugs are brought into the facility. You sure you don't want me to trail along with you inside?"

"That's okay. I don't want to spook Summers. We need answers. Michelle needs answers." Whitney glanced in the side mirror and spotted the Camaro parked behind them. "Besides, you can keep Mike company."

It felt weird being followed even though she knew who had her back. It certainly wasn't something she wanted to get used to.

While a security vehicle drove by making its rounds circling the property for the second time since they'd arrived, Whitney got out of the van. Security personnel had already searched their vehicles thoroughly inside and out. Afterward, they awarded each of them with security clearance badges allowing them to be on the premises.

After heading to a small security cottage manned by two armed guards, Whitney walked through an airport-style metal detector and her purse was put on a conveyor belt and checked through an x-ray scanner.

One of the guards with a square jaw and a deadpan expression on his face held out his hand. "Security clearance, please."

She handed the man the security badge.

"Any guns, weapons or explosives?"

She shook her head. "No."

He pushed a log book in front of her. "Sign in here."

Whitney signed the book and the guard handed her an identification card.

"Terry will walk you over to the lab to meet Mr. Summers."

Whitney followed the second guard out of the cottage and across the lawn to a separate building. Once inside the facility, Whitney had to pass through another security checkpoint complete with four armed guards, another metal detector and more questions about weapons and explosives. When she was finished, she was given a second identification card.

Dell Summers immediately met her wearing a loose gray button-down shirt and black pants. He was a thin man with shiny black hair and a dark tan. He appeared to be in his thirties, which was surprising considering the position he held at the lab.

Whitney shook his hand. "Thank you for seeing me on such short notice."

"My pleasure. Come with me."

He escorted her through etched glass doors that opened into an atrium with chocolate brown leather lounge chairs and luscious green plants. Soft music played from wall speakers in the corner of the room.

"Please. Have a seat."

Whitney pulled out her digital recorder from her purse, set it on the table between them and pressed the 'play' button. "Tell me more about Flatiron Sargasso and the type of work you do here."

He stared at the recorder, and then up at her. "The twelve-thousand-square-foot facility is less than a year old. The interior is built like a submarine with airtight and monitored pressurized space. We have both BSL-3 and BSL-4 labs on-site. We are one of only two BSL-4 labs in the country."

"How many people do you have on staff?"

"Ten assistants, support staff, and thirty-five scientists, many of which are doctorate-level trying to discover how virulent infectious diseases kill their hosts. They've made it their life mission. Dr. Fielding was one of our senior researchers."

"What was he working on?"

"He spent most of his time in the level four lab mainly working with Ebola, Marburg and other various killers that are transmissible and incurable. I can't tell you the exact nature of his research." The man paused for a long moment. "I was sorry to hear he died. He was a nice guy and respected by his colleagues."

Ebola? Marburg? Goosebumps skated across her skin under her jacket and she thought about Fielding and the two men at the warehouse. She forced herself to focus, to stay on track, to get the answers she needed. "What's— the difference between a BSL-3 and the BSL-4 lab?"

"The main difference is the type of pathogens researchers are allowed to study. For example, bubonic plague is at level three while Ebola and other lethal pathogens must be quarantined at level four."

"I know Flatiron Sargasso has had an impeccable safety record but is it possible for specimens to go missing?"

A spark of irritation flitted in his blue eyes at her question. "Are you insinuating something?"

"Not at all. I'm trying to understand what types of security measures are in place to make certain something like that never happens. You and I know both know we live in a much different world than we did prior to the Diablo Canyon Nuclear Plant attack and 9/11."

"I can't discuss specific security measures. I *can* assure you, our facility is more than secure to ensure every sample is accounted for. We have never had any inventory discrepancies."

"Have you ever had an incident where one of your scientists became infected with a sample they were working with?"

Part of being a reporter meant reading people. The man's body language spoke volumes, the way he kept crossing and uncrossing his arms over his chest. There was something he wasn't telling her.

"We've never had a situation like the one you have described and I hope we don't. Even if we did, we would be able to confine the problem immediately. Let me give you another example." He crossed his legs and leaned forward. "To enter the restricted BSL-4 lab a scientist would first have to go through two heavy stainless steel doors used as an airlock and would punch in the code which deactivates the magnetic lock on door number one. The airlock also houses the decontamination shower. The building's automation system is alerted the second the air pressure is about to change. Once the scientist enters the level four lab the automation system forces high-pressure air into the air flows and traps any airborne pathogens."

Now it seemed as if the man was working too hard to give her information by over explaining. Whitney wasn't buying it. "I think I have everything I need. I've taken up more than enough of your time." She stopped the recorder and put the device in her purse. "I want to thank you again for seeing me."

Summers stood and smiled. "If you need anything else, please feel free to contact me. I'll walk you out."

Whitney grabbed her purse and got up. Her eyes shifted to the air ducts in the ceiling as they walked out of the atrium to the main lobby. Her father's voice flooded her thoughts.

"Everyone has something to hide. You just have to look hard enough."

Something happened in this building with Matthew Fielding. Dell Summers knew it. So did Whitney.

CHAPTER FIVE

B lake arrived at the FBI field office on West Lake Mead Boulevard and squinted in the late afternoon sunlight. The hundred-thousand-square-foot building was a typical looking commercial property, bland and ordinary, not a building bustling with hundreds of agents, intelligence analysts, language specialists, scientists, information technology specialists, and support staff.

He needed to know what had happened at the warehouse.

Trent Chambers met him in the hallway outside his office with his silver hair slicked back and wearing his usual Bureau uniform, a navy suit, white shirt and dark red tie. "Go on in. I'll be right back."

Blake nodded and took a seat in front of the man's desk. He stared at the pictures littering the wall behind the desk of Chambers with officials he didn't know and various photographs of the man's family. If Fielding had been infected, anyone he had contact with could have been infected as well. Fear burrowed deep in his bones. The thought terrified him. An outbreak was the last thing the country needed especially after the terrorist attack at Diablo Canyon.

Minutes later, Chambers charged into the room with a

piece of paper in his hand and closed the door. "You have to see this."

Blake took the paper and read. It was Fielding's autopsy report. "A gunshot wound to the head? The guy was murdered?" He scanned the report. No mention of an infectious disease. Nothing.

"That's what the report says. He was murdered. I called the city morgue and was told his body wasn't there. No one knows where it is. I also called the CDC after you and I talked earlier and spoke with Don Greeden. He said he'd never heard of the scientist."

"What about the two men at the warehouse? Where are they? Are they still alive?"

"We have no clue. There's no record of them being taken to any of the area hospitals and they weren't brought to the morgue." Chambers paused then resumed. "I have to ask—but—is there a chance Mike and Whitney misinterpreted what they saw at the warehouse and all of this can be blamed on lost paperwork or someone forgetting to type the details into a computer system?"

"Definitely not. We have three missing bodies and no idea what's going on except that Fielding was murdered." He held up the paper. "We don't even know if this is true." He slapped the paper down on the desk and pulled a clear case containing a DVD from his shirt pocket and hurled it at the man. "Watch it. Then tell me Mike and Whitney are wrong."

Chambers huffed a grunt of annoyance and opened the case. He slid the disc into the DVD drive of his laptop.

While the warehouse video played, Blake watched the man, his gaze locked on the laptop screen. His bushy eyebrows raised, lowered, and raised again. His eyes widened and he looked up at Blake. "The CDC was there?"

"Enough evidence for you?"

"Why would the director of the CDC claim he knew nothing about Fielding when I called? Christ, I run the Las Vegas FBI field office. I should be in the loop."

Blake heard the fury in Chambers' voice. If it was one thing the man always hated was being kept in the dark. He liked, and needed, to be in control always. "That's not the most important question. What the hell do these men have that the CDC would go to such lengths to cover it up?"

The man shook his head. "I don't know. This isn't good."

No, it wasn't. "We could have a major outbreak on our hands and not even know it. Whitney's gone to speak with the man who runs the lab where Fielding worked. Hopefully, she learns something."

Chambers loosened his tie. "I'll put a call into Homeland Security and let them know what's going on. Better safe than sorry at this point."

"We have another problem. This one affects you as well." Blake leaned forward in the chair and rested his elbows on his knees. "Nathan Shaw is demanding to see Angel."

"For Christ sakes. That is the last thing anyone needs including the kid."

"If I don't agree to let him see her, he's threatened to contact the media and tell them that she's the world's first cloned human."

Silence electrified the room.

"It's your call." Chambers glanced out the window, and then back to him. "I'll support whatever you decide."

That was a first. Usually, Blake had to fight like hell to get the man to support anything.

"Any idea what you're going to do?"

"No."

"Let me know when you do."

There was concern in the man's voice. Blake understood. His former SAC needed a heads-up because of the potential fallout if the information about Angel was leaked. Not only had Blake covered up the information, so had Chambers and that was enough to get the man fired and the both of them thrown in jail for concealing evidence.

"I also discovered a connection between Shaw and the lab where Fielding worked."

Chambers' eyes widened for the second time. "Is it enough for us to bring him in?"

Blake shook his head. "I wish it was. He donated a large sum of money to Fielding's lab while he was locked up."

"The guy's like an insect you can't kill. If you need more resources let me know."

Blake wanted to squash Shaw under his shoe once and for all. For now, he could only dream of the day when Nathan Shaw was finally out of their lives and he hoped it was soon.

As the man sped the black Lexus down the highway northeast of Vegas, his cell phone rang. He grunted under his breath and checked the clock on the dash. Four-forty-five. He was already running late. He was supposed to be in the lab to ensure things were moving forward as planned with the new virus. He eased his foot off the gas pedal and steered the sedan onto the side of the road and stopped. He grabbed his phone off the passenger seat. "Yes."

"We might have a problem."

"What is it?"

"The reporter just left Flatiron Sargasso."

He understood the woman was doing her job, but they didn't need her nosing around and getting too close—at least not yet. "We must be cautious. I've learned from an inside source at the CDC that the scientist's body has been transferred to an undisclosed location. It won't be long before their own scientists figure out what has happened. Then the news will be out. I'm guessing soon."

His contact would not be happy. No one was supposed to discover the scientist's body for days. That's why the warehouse was chosen. It was supposed to be the perfect location. Everything needed to run smoothly for all involved—more importantly on schedule.

"Keep an eye on the woman. Let me know where she goes and who she talks to. We need to be one step ahead of her."

"She has what you call in America, an escort. A man driving a red Camaro. He might be ex-military."

He made a mental note to find out who the man was. "It might be time to give the woman and her escort a bit of a warning."

The man knew his new-found friend did things much differently in his own country. If he wanted to send a warning, people were burned alive, blown up or executed by a bullet in the head. It was the only effective way to send a clear message—but not in this case.

"Remember she must not be harmed. I'll leave it up to you as to how you want to proceed. That's your expertise. Not mine."

His thoughts turned to the men at the warehouse he had disposed of. He'd surprisingly shown his own strength and expertise when needed. He'd gotten the job done. That's all that mattered. "No need to worry, my friend. In a few more days everything will come to an end." He checked his side mirror. "The reporter and her husband have no clue what is coming."

❄ ❄ ❄

Whitney arrived home a little after five and unlocked the front door of their three-bedroom ranch style house. Her conversation with Dell Summers played over in her mind. She needed to find out what he was hiding. The second she opened the door, Angel ran to her, her blonde curls bouncing with each pounding thump on the hardwood floor.

"You're—back."

Whitney bent and picked her up. "I missed you."

"I missed you more." She kissed Whitney's cheek.

"How was school?"

"We got to make a storybook."

"I can't wait to read your story."

"It's not done. Tomorrow or the next day the teacher said."

She spotted Blake in the living room speaking with his father. His mother, Carol, was sitting on the couch next to Sofia who was reading a beauty magazine. The young woman was beautiful in a movie-star-kind-of-way dressed in a soft pink tracksuit with her long dark brown hair pulled up in a high ponytail.

"How about you go play for a little bit before supper?" Whitney put Angel down.

The child's round blue eyes shone with mischief. She gave an animated nod and skipped down the hallway toward her bedroom at the back of the house. Once Angel was out of sight, Whitney entered the living room and uneasiness washed over her. The words Ebola and Marburg kept running through her head and the thought scared her to death.

Blake grinned the second he saw her. He wrapped his arm around the small of her back and kissed her temple. "I'm glad you're home."

For a second the uneasiness vanished and she felt safe. It didn't last long. "Me too." Whitney glanced at his father. "Thanks for picking Angel up after school."

"Anytime. She's one smart kid and a pleasure to have around. She makes us feel young again."

Blake's mother smiled. "We're more than happy to, dear."

Whitney didn't want to do this in front of Sofia but she was old enough to understand what was going on. "We need to talk. All of us."

Blake held her a little closer to his body giving her the support and reassurance she needed.

"What's going on?" Blake's father asked.

A tight, anxious feeling filled her throat as if the air was being squeezed out of her lungs. Whitney inhaled a deep breath and let it out slowly. "We found out Nathan Shaw was released on bail today."

His father frowned as if expecting to hear something else. His jaw tightened. "Son, how did this happen?"

"He more than likely paid off a few people including his lawyer and a judge. It's what he always does." He stopped for a moment. "There is some good news, though. We don't have to worry about the cartel anymore. Alejandro Quintero is dead."

"That's great news, son. Thank God."

She witnessed relief and hope in Sofia's brown eyes.

With Alejandro dead, the young woman knew her mother, Mariana, would be safe in Panama and perhaps in time she would be able to visit her.

"Everyone still needs to be super cautious. We still have Shaw to worry about. He has nothing to lose and will do anything to destroy this family. He's proved that over the years."

His mother winced at his words and nervously wrung her hands in her lap.

"Is that why someone was following me today?" Sofia asked.

"Yes. Paul McBride. I guess you noticed him."

She gave Blake a small smile. "It really wasn't hard to spot him. He's a big man."

Sofia was right. Paul McBride was six-foot-three and built like a grizzly bear. He was a hard man to miss even in a crowd.

"He's an FBI agent. You met him at the wedding. He'll keep you safe while you're at school. For now, until things settle down it might be wise to stick to just school and home. I know it's a lot to ask. I'll give you his cell phone number later in case you need it. Use it if you feel threatened in any way even if it's just a gut feeling."

The young woman set the magazine on the coffee table. "I will."

More than anything Whitney wanted to talk about what she'd learned at Flatiron Sargasso but she didn't want to worry Blake's parents or Sofia anymore than they already were. The news of Nathan Shaw was a heavy enough burden for any of them to digest.

"Son, I think your mother and I should take Angel away for a while until things settle down. I don't want to see the child in that man's crosshairs again. There's no telling what he'll do next." His watery eyes shifted to Sofia. "You're more than welcome to join us. We'd love to have you."

"Thank you but I'm already a month behind this semester. I can't miss any more of my classes. Do I have to go, Blake?"

"No. No one is going anywhere, at least not yet. We'll figure this out if and when we need to."

Sofia stood and placed the magazine on the coffee table. "I'm going to start dinner if that's okay."

"You know you don't have to make supper for us all the time," Whitney said.

"I know I don't. I really enjoy it. I have a culinary exam next week so I need the practice."

She smiled and watched Sofia head to the kitchen. She'd never met a young woman so motivated and inspiring at the same time. She could tell Sofia was still putting on a brave face mourning the loss of her father. There was always a defined sadness in the back of her eyes even when there was a smile on her face.

Whitney felt Blake grasp her hand.

"You guys are more than welcome to stay for dinner."

"Thanks for the invite but your mother and I have other plans. We're meeting our neighbors at Burger Brasserie. It's a weekly thing we do." Frank's eyes shifted toward the kitchen and lowered his voice to almost a whisper. "Maybe it's time to take matters into our own hands, son. At least that horrible man would be out of lives for good."

Blake's mother gave her husband a worried look as she got up from the couch. "Frank, you're not suggesting—"

"I am. Someone needs to take him out. There I said it."

Whitney was surprised Frank would suggest killing

Nathan. It seemed out of character considering his background.

"Believe me. I have considered it," Blake said.

Whitney wasn't startled by her husband's response. They'd endured so much loss because of Nathan Shaw.

"Let's go, Carol. We don't want to be late." He patted his son on the shoulder. "Think about it."

After Blake's parents left, Whitney collapsed on the couch. While Sofia was busy in the kitchen, she heard giggling coming from Angel's bedroom. The child was always happy and able to keep herself entertained for hours on end.

Blake sat beside her and put his arm around her shoulder. "We're finally alone."

She cuddled closer grateful to have a little time together before dinner. "Your father was serious, wasn't he?"

"My father never says something he doesn't mean. Being a career Marine taught him that, retired or not."

"You're not going to—"

"No. I'm not prepared to lose what I have." He leaned his head against hers. "We have to find another way to make sure Shaw stays out of our lives for good which means getting him back where he belongs on death row."

Whitney sat forward, and their gazes met. "I'm worried sick. I found out Dr. Fielding was working with Ebola and Marburg. I'm also sure Dell Summers at Flatiron Sargasso is hiding something. Something happened at the lab and he's covering it up."

"Jesus. Then we possibly do have an outbreak on our hands. When I spoke to Chambers earlier, he said Fielding's body was missing as well as the two men from the warehouse. No clue if the men are dead or alive. We believe the CDC have them."

She saw the concern on his face and a shiver rocketed down her spine. An outbreak? If the men were infected, why hadn't the CDC alerted the public? She made a mental note to contact the CDC and Fielding's family in the morning. Then she saw something else in Blake's eyes. "There's something you aren't telling me."

He paused almost looking as if he was searching for the right words. "Nathan Shaw called me this morning."

This can't be happening again. Whitney was almost afraid to ask. "What did he want?"

"He's demanding to see Angel."

"What? No. We can't let that happen, Blake. He has no legal right to see her."

"We might not have a choice. It's not about the law. It's about what Shaw will do if we don't agree. This could affect both of us and Angel, as well as the Bureau. We need to talk to Kurtz first thing tomorrow."

"I don't believe this." Panic and anger filled her voice and she forced herself to calm down. "He's threatening to go public about Angel, isn't he?"

"He said he would." Blake rubbed his forehead. "I have no reason not to believe him. He's made good on every threat as long as we've known him."

"What are we going to do? We can't let him see her."

"I don't know. We're going to have to figure it out. The more I think about it, it might be a good idea to let my parents take Angel away especially with a risk of a possible outbreak. It's up to Sofia if she wants to go. She's eighteen, old enough to decide for herself." He pulled her back toward him and wrapped his arms around her holding her tight. "We're going to have to tell Sofia everything. There is more."

"As if everything that has happened so far isn't enough?"

"Shaw knew what color of wedding dress you were wearing. He made a point to tell me it was cream-colored."

She heard herself gasp and she choked back her disbelief. "He had someone inside our wedding?"

Blake nodded. "Do you still have the wedding guest list?"

"It's in the top drawer of your desk in the office." She started to get up.

"I'll get it."

When he returned, he handed her the list and sat back down.

She scanned the names on the list. "No one on here would do Nathan's dirty work."

"He had to have paid off one of the waiters or hotel staff."

For the third time, all Whitney could do was sit and watch her life crumbling down around her because of Nathan Shaw. She wondered if Blake's father was right. Maybe someone needs to take the man out.

CHAPTER SIX

T he next morning, rays of sunshine sparked across the horizon and spread lazily across the dark morning sky. Blake took the last sip of his coffee and finished going through the stack of paperwork on his desk desperately needing his attention. The heavy weight on his chest last night had lifted. At least Whitney was aware of Shaw's threat about exposing Angel. The last thing the kid needed was the media involved. His gut twisted. Their lives would turn into a circus unless Kurtz came up with something fast otherwise they wouldn't have any choice other than to give into Nathan's demand.

He'd already called Chambers and had woken him up to see if he had learned anything new since yesterday about Fielding and the men at the warehouse. Nothing. No one was talking—especially not the CDC. He wished like hell he knew exactly what they were dealing with. His cell phone rang and startled him. He retrieved the phone from his T-shirt pocket and recognized the caller ID. It was Michelle, a call he was dreading. He took a deep breath and let it out. "Hi, Michelle."

"Have you learned anything about my uncle? It's driving us crazy not knowing what happened to him."

"I was just about to call you." He lied. He couldn't

tell her that her uncle was probably infected with some deadly disease because he had no actual proof. "All we know right now is—he was shot."

"Shot?"

He heard a gasp on the other end.

"Why would someone shoot him? He was the most caring and kind man in the world. I don't understand. I just don't."

Her voice broke and it sounded as if she was going to cry. He hated doing this, delivering bad news. In all his years with the Bureau, it never got easier.

Blake wished he had the answers, but he didn't, and that left a bitter taste in his mouth. "I don't know but I promise you I'll find out. The investigation is just in the beginning stages. I'll call you as soon as I know more. I really am sorry, Michelle. I know how hard this is."

"Thank you for doing this for me and my family." Sadness filled her voice. "Please find out what happened to him."

"I will. You have my word." He ended the call thankful the conversation was done for now.

The buzzer at the back door of SecuraCorp went off. He typed a half-dozen keystrokes into the keyboard of his laptop and checked the security camera. It was Hal, his ex-marine buddy, and former FBI agent. He'd called him late last night. Blake jumped out of his chair and rushed to the back of the office hallway to let him in.

"Hey, Decker. Thanks for coming. Good to see you."

Hal was a big guy; six-two and two-hundred and thirty pounds of pure muscle. He had his blond hair cut "high and tight"—marine style, much shorter than the last time he'd seen him when he'd helped Blake rescue Whitney in Colombia.

"Anytime." Hal handed him an extra-large coffee. "I'm guessing you could use another one of these this morning."

Blake took the coffee, thankful for a second cup. "Thanks, man." He pulled the heavy metal door shut and double checked the lock.

After the two men settled in the office, Blake told Hal about the scientist, and what had happened at the warehouse.

Hal looked at him with hard blue eyes. "Christ. There could be people out there walking around not even knowing they're infected and infecting others. Man, I thought the terrorist attack at the nuclear plant was scary. This could really blossom into a large-scale outbreak if we don't get ahead of it, and quickly."

"We do need to get ahead of it. There are a few problems. The main one being the CDC is covering up the incident. I have no idea why. Also, it looks like Nathan Shaw might be involved." Blake went on and told Hal what he had found.

"You're probably right. He's probably in a lot deeper than just donating some cash. That asshole just doesn't know when to quit." Hal leaned back in the chair and stretched his legs. "You know I can look after him quickly and efficiently."

"I would never ask you to do that. This isn't your problem, Hal."

"You don't have to ask. Just give the word."

Blake was aware of his friend's skills. Hal was a crack shot with a sniper rifle. One of the best with close to a hundred kills during their time in the Marines. That didn't include kills during covert assignments off-the-books while he was with the FBI or afterward. He'd been awarded a Silver Star Medal and numerous Bronze Star Medals along with other various unit and personal awards. One shot and Shaw would be out of their lives for good. It sure sounded good. Blake had to admit he was tempted.

"We need to bug Shaw's house."

"No problem."

"It won't be easy. He's under house arrest so we'll have to come up with a plan to get him out of the house so we can get in. We need a way for the judge to sign off to allow him to leave the premise for a medical appointment or an emergency."

"I can look after it. How about a non-lethal shot? It's not as if the guy doesn't deserve it. He sure-as-hell deserves a lot more. He's pissed off a lot of people over the years."

Blake thought about it. The idea did give him a bit of satisfaction knowing Shaw would suffer. It was probably the only way to get him out of the house. He was also confident Hal would cover his tracks, something else he was an expert at. "Non-lethal."

"You got it. When do you want it done?"

"Tomorrow after dark." Blake handed him a piece of paper with an address written on it. "I'll meet you there."

Hal nodded and stuffed the paper in his pocket. He took a gulp of his coffee. "I have a special bullet with his name on it. Are you sure you want it non-lethal?"

"Yeah." For now, Blake wanted to add but stopped himself.

"I think it would beneficial to have Angela Donahue involved in case you're right about the outbreak. We don't know who or what we're up against. The more people working on this the better."

Blake agreed. "Call her in."

Hal grabbed his coffee cup and rose to his feet. "If you change your mind about Shaw, let me know. A shot is a shot. Just depends on how you want it served up."

* * *

An hour after Hal left his office, Blake steered the F-150 pickup truck onto the off ramp and sped past McCarran International Airport twenty minutes south of Las Vegas. To the west, the sky was streaked in violent shades of gray and reflected his mood. A storm was brewing in more ways than one.

From the search he'd done at the office he learned the property Shaw had rented was on Club Vista Drive overlooking the country club's luxury golf course in Henderson at the base of the Black Mountains. The main three-storey house was twelve thousand square feet with seven bedrooms, nine bathrooms, pool, spa, and a six-car garage. The bastard must have felt as if he died and went to heaven living in a mansion after sitting on death row at Nevada State Prison in Carson City.

Five minutes later, he turned right onto Anthem Club Drive. To the left was the pristine golf course with a handful of early birds deciding to get in a game before the workday began. By the looks of the neighborhood and the multi-million-dollar houses, Hal was going to have a problem finding a secluded area without alarming neighbors of his presence. He spotted Joe Cally jogging up the road leading to Shaw's temporary home. He slowed the vehicle and stopped on the side of the road.

Cally halted when he saw him, bent over, and placed his hands on his thighs clearly working to catch his breath. A few minutes later, he whisked the moisture from his forehead with his hand.

Blake rolled down the window. Hot dry air filled the interior of the truck and clashed with the cool air streaming from the vents. "Why the hell are you jogging?"

"No choice. Security wasn't happy I was making the rounds in my vehicle. You know how these security companies can be. They think they're cops or something and own the area." He blew out a chest full of air and patted his stomach. "Besides, I could use a little exercise."

Blake looked up the road and his pulse sped up. "Anything going on?"

"I haven't seen Shaw's lawyer yet today, but the day is young. Other than a catering truck delivering food about ten minutes ago, it's been quiet. It's going to be tough getting video without anyone noticing especially with private security driving around every few hours." He glanced at his watch. "They're due again soon."

"Get whatever video and photos you can." Blake quickly filled Cally in about Hal and their plan to get Shaw out of the house. "We're going to need your help. You're going to have to flash your FBI credentials around."

"No problem. I'm in."

"Have you seen Shaw outside at all?"

"He came out yesterday and was wandering around at the front of the property. Later I caught him sitting by the pool in the back. I was able to snag some video with my phone. I had to climb up there." He raised a hand and shielded his eyes against the sun's glare and pointed to a man-made cliff designed with large jutted rocks, green foliage, and large cactuses. "It circles the entire perimeter of the neighborhood."

It was the perfect spot for their entry point. "Good to know. I'm going to do a drive by and check the place out."

If Blake saw Shaw, he wasn't sure what he'd do. There were years of pent up anger inside him for everything the man had done especially for killing his sister and helping to kidnap Whitney. Not to mention shooting him, and now threatening to expose Angel to the media.

As if reading his mind, Cally said, "Are you sure that's a good idea?"

Blake shrugged. "I just want to see where he's living. Keep me updated. I'll have Hal call you later on." He put the truck in drive and rolled forward.

"Don't be doing anything stupid."

He wasn't convinced he wouldn't do something that could get him arrested and that scared him. It was different when the Shaw was in behind bars. Now that he was out, all bets were off. His eyes roamed to the rear-view mirror and he noticed a black security vehicle parked at the bottom of the hill.

An eighth of a mile up the road, Blake pulled in front of Shaw's house and stopped.

Fifty-foot palm trees lined both sides of the driveway, their broad fronds swaying in the wind. The place looked like a palace with towering thick white columns, floor to ceiling windows, dozens of walkout balconies, and landscaping probably costing a small fortune to maintain on a regular basis.

Anger seethed inside him and he clutched the steering wheel until his fingers hurt. He spotted Shaw sauntering across the lush bluish-green lawn as if he didn't have a care in the world. He appeared frail, the way his shoulders slumped forward. He didn't look like the same man Blake had worked for at ShawBioGen. But he was the same killer, now living like a king.

Hatred sliced through him and his pulse slammed at his temples. He threw the truck in park and popped open the glove box. As he stared at his gun, perspiration beaded along his upper lip. He'd been forced to kill in the past to defend his country, himself, and Whitney. Not in cold blood. Not like this.

Seconds ticked by.

Blake grabbed the .40 caliber Glock 22 from the glove box and felt the virtual line he was about to cross. His finger touched the safety on the trigger and he thought about Whitney, Sofia, and Angel.

If he did this, he would lose them—give up everything. He pulled back the slide and chambered a round. Fear, raw and strangling, clawed up his throat. His mouth went dry. If he didn't, Nathan Shaw would never be out of their lives. At least his family would be safe. He reached for the door handle.

A horn blared twice.

Every muscle in Blake's body tensed.

A black security car pulled up beside his truck.

"Hey. You lost?" a male driver asked.

Blake looked away not wanting to watch Shaw a second longer. He pushed the weapon under his thigh and hung his head out the window forced to focus his attention on the security guy. "I—think so. I was looking for a friend. I think I have the wrong house."

"What's your friend's name?"

Blake lied for the second time today. "James McMaster."

The man paused and rubbed his forehead. "I know everyone in the neighborhood. I've never heard of him."

"My secretary must have written down the wrong address. Thanks for your help." He shifted the truck into drive and forced a smile. "Have a good day."

Little did the driver know, he'd saved him from doing something stupid. Nathan Shaw wasn't worth losing his family or his life. Blake opened the glove box and placed the Glock inside, and then stomped the gas pedal determined to get as far away as possible before he changed his mind.

* * *

Jason Kratz sat behind his desk and passed Whitney a legal document. "Shaw's attorney is prepared to file this later morning." She read the document and handed it to Blake. Nerves jangled, and fear touched the back of her throat. Nathan wanted custody of Angel. It wasn't as if they didn't have enough to worry about with a possible outbreak. Now the man was coming after an innocent little girl. "How can he do this?"

"He has no legal right to the child under the law. That doesn't mean he can't file whatever he wants." Flipping through some notes, the frown on his face deepened. "He could try to use the fact it was his technology used to replicate an identical copy of Blake's sister's DNA. He could also use the fact he had the child in his custody for the first couple of years. It's pretty far-fetched as far as the realms of the law are concerned, but it's something he'll try."

Whitney believed Jason was right. Nathan would use anything he possibly could to try to get custody of Angel.

"I guess I shouldn't have told him to fuck off when he called. The media is going to have a field day with this if it gets out."

Her stomach flip-flopped, and she heard the undeniable strain in Blake's voice. "It's not going to matter what we do. Nathan is going public and this is the way he's doing it."

"I agree. We need to be proactive. Who else knows about Angel? I need names."

Blake rattled off four names of FBI agents including Trent Chambers, as well as two high-up officials in the Justice Department.

His words slithered through her brain and her thoughts turned to her ex-husband.

Her gaze snapped to Mason, lying on his back. Dark red blood pumped from a gaping wound in his chest, soaking his white shirt. A knot wedged in her throat, one she couldn't swallow. "I'm going to get help."

"No—stay." Blood bubbled at the corners of his mouth and trickled down his jaw. "They cloned..."

An icy chill drove through her body and brought her back to the present. So many people who knew the truth were already dead. Nathan had made sure of it.

"Does Sofia know?" the DA asked.

"We've—" Her voiced cracked. "Never had a reason to tell her."

The DA looked at Blake. "What about your parents?"

"Yes. They pretty much know everything."

Whitney stared at the framed photograph hanging on the wall of the DA's young daughter, an angelic-looking toddler with chubby cheeks, and forced herself to ask even though the idea frightened her. "Do you think if we allow him to see her he will back off?"

"It might be a short-term solution and buy us some time while we search deeper into his dealings with Flatiron Sargasso Laboratories."

Blake threw the document on the desk. "This is bull-shit. It's just another low-life blackmail move on Shaw's part. I can guarantee his so-called donation is as dirty as he is."

"I would advise you both to seriously consider it. We all know the situation involves others, not just you, Whitney and Angel."

"I know, Jason. I'm not about to watch Trent Chambers or the others go down for this. Whitney and I included, and then we'd lose Angel for good. Careers and lives are on the line."

"That's exactly what he wants. For us to lose. We're not going to." She looked at Blake, and then to the Jason. "We have to do this. We don't have a choice."

Tense silence stretched across the room.

"Set it up." Blake's jaw twitched. "I want you present, Jason."

"I don't know if Shaw will—."

Blake stood and shoved his chair back forcefully. "Just do what you can."

After finishing their meeting with Kurtz, Whitney stopped in the hallway outside the DA's office. She had never seen Blake look or sound so defeated. What worried her more was he might kill Nathan himself. A pang of fear twisted in her stomach and formed a hard knot. She turned and faced him. "Promise me you won't do anything to Nathan."

He stared at her, his features suddenly soft and slack. "I promise. I can't guarantee someone else won't get to him. It's not as if the man hasn't made a lot of enemies."

Whitney knew how much easier their lives would be without Nathan Shaw in it but she wasn't prepared to lose her husband. There had already been too much loss in her life. She searched his brown eyes praying he was telling the truth.

He'd always had a poker face from the time she'd met him. It came with the territory working for the FBI. Over time Whitney had learned to recognize the signs, like a quick flicker in the back of his eyes as if he wanted to look away. She didn't see anything. She shrugged off the dark thoughts and slipped her hand into his. "I've got to get back to the station. I want to do some more research into Matthew Fielding and Flatiron Sargasso. I know there's an answer buried somewhere and I'm going to find it."

"I have to meet with Hal later and everyone is meeting at the house tonight. Hal and Angela included. We need a plan. I'm not comfortable knowing the scientist was infected with some unknown deadly disease and we still don't know what it is, or if anyone else has been infected besides the men at the warehouse."

Neither was she. They desperately needed to know for all their sakes.

He glanced at his watch. "I've got to get back to the office even though I'd rather hang out with my beautiful wife." His cell phone went off.

The high-pitched chirps played on her nerves and made her flinch.

He pulled the phone from the back pocket of his jeans and checked the text message. Worry lines spread across his forehead. "Mike's car broke down. He said he'd be about an hour." He typed in a short message. "I told him to meet you at the station. I'm not happy not having someone with you. I could call one of my US marshal friends."

"No. It's okay. Don't worry. I'll be fine. It's only for an hour."

Two female legal clerks strolled by quietly chatting back and forth.

With boyish hesitation, Blake kissed her cheek. "Let's get out of here."

As they walked out of the building her thoughts turned to Nathan and how they'd been manipulated again. The sonofabitch had gotten what he wanted. A chance to see Angel. Whitney just hoped they were doing the right thing because Nathan Shaw always wanted more—and it always ended with blood.

CHAPTER SEVEN

After their meeting with the DA, Whitney returned to the news station and found the usual bustling space abnormally quiet. Travis was nowhere to be found, and her assistant said Jerry had just left to do a quick errand.

She sat behind her desk, her nerves still on edge at the thought of Nathan seeing Angel. Whitney was terrified to be in the same room with the man. Who could blame her? He'd killed everyone in her life she cared about and had almost killed the man she loved. She had to find a way to prove Nathan's involvement, that his donation to Flatiron Sargasso Laboratories was a front for something much bigger and deadlier. An outbreak. She might be able to even stop his ridiculous custody threat. Getting him back in prison would make a judge think twice about his insane claim, at least she prayed it would, of course, if he didn't pay off another judge. Whitney had to figure this out for Angel's sake. She wasn't going to lose the little girl. Just because they had agreed to allow Nathan to see the child, he wouldn't stop there. He'd want another visit and another. It would never be enough. It would never end.

She opened her laptop determined to find a way to stop him and it would begin by discovering if he had financial dealings with any other labs in the US or abroad. As she searched database after database an hour flew by and she came up empty. She popped a piece of blueberry muffin in her mouth and downed it with the last sip of the tea she'd picked up at the corner Starbucks. Whitney typed in 'BSL-3 labs' plus 'ShawBioGen' into the browser's search bar and did an Internet search hoping to find labs associated with Nathan.

Nothing.

She tried again using 'BSL-4 labs' and 'ShawBioGen'.

Then she got a hit. She straightened in the chair and read the article.

At first, she thought her eyes were deceiving her. Nathan had made another donation. Twenty-five-million-dollars to Genomics BioMedical in San Antonio, Texas six months ago, while he was in prison. The Genomics website stated the lab dealt mainly with smallpox and Ebola. Anger bubbled inside her and fear festered and wouldn't let go. Why was he donating large sums of money to multiple labs? One lab she could see as a coincidence. Two. Not a chance. She knew the man well enough to know he wasn't giving away money out of the goodness of his heart. He was getting something in return. Something he desperately needed.

Whitney glanced across the room at the glass corner cabinet displaying the numerous the awards she'd collected over the years and to the Emmy she'd won for her story on human cloning immediately after Nathan was arrested. Her gaze shifted back to her desk to the photograph of her father. His words echoed through her head. *"You just have to look hard enough."*

On a hunch, she ran another search, this time looking to see if any scientists had died in Texas in the past three months. After a few seconds, her eyes widened. James Nova. Fifty-four years old. She kept reading. "Oh, my—."

"Hey. What's going on?" Jerry strolled into her office and plonked down on the couch.

"You won't believe this. One sec. I've got to call Blake." She retrieved her cell phone out from her purse and hit speed dial. After a few rings, he answered.

"Hi, baby."

The moment she heard his voice she couldn't contain her shock of what she had found. "I just learned Nathan donated twenty-five-million dollars to another lab, one in Texas."

"Two labs? What is he up to?"

"I don't know but I found more." She glanced at Jerry, then back to her laptop screen. "I did another search and discovered a scientist by the name of James Nova died under suspicious circumstances the day before Matthew Fielding. He was found dead in his car from a gunshot to his head but the weapon that killed him was discovered in the locked glove box of his vehicle."

"Jesus. The bodies linked to Shaw are starting to pile up."

"By the looks of it, Nathan has no connection to any other labs. This sure can't be a coincidence, can it? Two scientists murdered from BSL-4 labs in two different states?"

"It's not a coincidence. Shaw is up to no good. I'll see if I can find out more on my end and we'll talk to Chambers tonight. Good work. I'll see you at home. Love you and be careful. We both know Shaw. The moment we get too close, someone dies."

Whitney knew that all too well. After the call ended, she looked at Jerry.

Her cameraman shook his head. "I'm not surprised one bit after everything Nathan Shaw has done in the past."

She wasn't either, but they still had no idea what Nathan was up to. "Would you mind getting me another tea from across the street? I have a couple more calls to make, and afterward, I'll figure out what you and I are going to do today."

"Sure." He got up from the couch and walked to the door then stopped. "Oh. Travis said he needed an update tomorrow."

Whitney nodded. "Where is he?"

"No idea. I spoke with him earlier. He said he had some personal things to look after and he'd be in later."

It was odd her boss wasn't at the station. As long as she'd been working at News3 she only remembered Travis taking one day off. He was always here. "Okay. Thanks."

While Jerry went to get her a tea, Whitney called the CDC hoping to talk to the director. After waiting on hold for five minutes it wasn't surprising when she received an angry, 'he's not available' from his secretary. Next, she left a message with her contact at the Las Vegas Police Department asking if she could get a copy of James Nova's police report.

Whitney leaned back in the chair and rubbed the back of her neck for a few moments trying to help relieve some of the stress of the past couple of days. One way or another she was going to figure out what was going on. She picked up her cell phone again and dialed Matthew Fielding's number she'd gotten from his police report.

A woman answered after the third ring. "Hello?"

"Hi. Is this Janet Fielding?"

"Who is this?"

"My name is Whitney Steel. Your niece, Michelle, works for my husband at SecuraCorp."

"Oh, yes. I know who you are. You're a reporter."

"I just wanted to send my condolences. I was sorry to hear about your husband."

"Thank you. I appreciate that."

"This is going to sound a bit odd. Did your husband act or say anything to you that you thought was off before his death?"

"I don't know anything. Matthew went to work at the lab like usual. He called me at lunch like he usually does. The next call I got was from the police saying they had found his body in some warehouse."

"Was anything unusual about his call at lunch time?"

"He said—like I said. I don't know anything. I really need to go. Thanks for calling."

The line went dead.

Michelle's aunt knew a lot more than she was saying. She was about to say something and changed her mind. Or someone changed it for her. The conversation sounded rehearsed as if someone was telling her exactly what to say. Whitney's mind raced. What if she knew what her husband was infected with? What if Janet and her daughter, Scarlet, were infected and they needed medical attention? Whitney was astounded the CDC hadn't already swooped in and moved the woman and her daughter to a secure location. She needed to speak to Janet again before the CDC did.

She spun the chair around and stared out the window. Her thoughts shifted to Michelle. Blake's secretary was due back in the office the day after tomorrow. She imagined Michelle already knew her uncle's body was missing. For now, they couldn't allow her return to work until they were certain she wasn't exposed.

"Here's your tea."

"Thanks."

"Everything okay?"

Whitney turned the chair and faced Jerry. "I need you to do something and bring the camera."

"Okay. What do you have in mind?"

"I want you to go to 16451 Greencreek Drive and drive around at least two blocks in each direction while filming the fronts of the houses and any cars parked in driveways, or on the street." She snatched her car keys out of her purse and threw them to him. "Take my car."

He caught the keys in mid-air. "What am I looking for?"

"Anything or anyone that looks out of place."

"I'll get packed up and head out."

"Thanks. Oh. If you see me at that address keep on driving."

He raised an eyebrow obviously baffled.

"I'll explain later. Trust me on this."

* * *

In the station's parking lot, Whitney spotted Mike leaning against a late model black Ford Focus. The vehicle looked like a plastic toy car compared to his usual muscle car. "I guess the Camaro is still in the shop?"

"Yeah. I should slip by the garage and pick it up. It needed more work than they first thought. Where are you headed?"

She hesitated, knowing he would probably try to stop her. He wasn't going to. "To talk to Fielding's wife."

"That's not a good idea at all. What if she has what

the scientist has?" He shook his head. "Blake is going to be pissed off. There is no way you are going inside the woman's house."

"This is my call, Mike. He can be angry with me. There are too many unanswered questions and I believe the woman knows what's going on. You don't have to worry. I won't go in the house. I have a plan and you're a part of it."

"Wonderful. I guess we're taking this beauty." He slapped his hand on the roof of the car. "I ran into Jerry. He just left."

She heard the sarcasm in his voice and smiled. Whitney knew she was putting him in an awkward position since his job was to protect her. She wasn't making it easy. If he was going to follow her around he'd have to come along for the ride. Mike didn't have a choice especially after her conversation with Michelle's aunt and learning another scientist had been murdered.

Whitney opened the car door. "We need to make a few stops on the way."

* * *

After Whitney bought a throw-away phone, flower arrangement, and a sympathy card, Mike parked on the other side of the street in front of Fielding's house on Greencreek Drive. She noticed a small compact car and RV parked in the driveway. Someone was home.

The house was a pleasant looking two-tone brown single storey home with a white metal fence surrounding the front yard peppered with striped plants resembling zebra print, cacti and gorgeous flowers in deep shades of purple, yellow and gold.

"Here comes Jerry." Whitney watched her cameraman drive past slowly in her car.

"What's he up to?"

"Checking the area for anyone who doesn't fit in."

Mike undid his seatbelt. "Are you sure this is going to work?"

She punched her name and phone number into the throw-away phone. "I hope so. It's all we can do right now. After talking to Fielding's wife, I believe she's being watched and possibly someone is listening to her phone conversations." She held up the flower arrangement. "This way it just looks like I'm dropping off the flowers because of her husband's death. Nothing out of the ordinary under the circumstances." After signing the card, she tucked the phone in the flower arrangement along with the card. "We have to try. She knows something and whatever that is could help us put the puzzle pieces together before more people die."

"You're not going to go in the house, right? Because I will tackle you. Don't think I won't."

She knew Mike would. He was always true to his word. "I promise." Her gaze wandered to the front door painted a glossy blood red. She spotted Jerry in the side mirror driving up the street. After he drove by, she opened the door and got out of the car.

Mike raised an eyebrow. "Be careful."

Clutching the flower arrangement in one arm, Whitney opened the gate and walked to the door. She set the flowers on the small porch at the base of the door and rapped three times. She turned and rushed back to the gate to make sure she wouldn't have any physical contact with the woman.

A few seconds passed and an attractive woman in her early fifties with porcelain skin and flaming red hair cut in a chic hairstyle opened the door. She stepped outside.

"I'm Whitney. I spoke with you earlier, Mrs. Fielding. I just wanted to drop those flowers off. It's important that I got them to you." She pointed to the woman's feet and stared at the container filled with colorful snapdragons, lilies, chrysanthemums, and carnations. "Again, I'm very sorry about your husband. My condolences to you and your daughter." She jerked her head toward the flowers. "They're important."

The woman remained silent with a look of confusion and apprehension on her face. She finally picked up the flowers. Before going back inside, she peered up and down the street as if she was looking for something or someone.

Whitney opened the car door and hopped in, convinced someone had eyes on the Janet Fielding. She scanned the street in both directions and only saw two empty cars parked on the side of the street.

Mike started the engine and put the car in drive. "There's no doubt she's being watched."

Whitney nodded. "At least she didn't appear sick but we still don't know for sure." She pulled on the seatbelt and locked it in place. "Hopefully, whoever is tracking her turns up in the video Jerry is taking. All we can do now is to wait for the woman to call. I believe she will."

Mike nodded and turned left onto E. Washington Ave and opened his window. "The mechanic's shop is a few blocks from here on Sandhill Road. I really need to ditch this thing."

Warm spring-like desert air engulfed the car and felt good against Whitney's face. The car really wasn't Mike's style. From the first time she'd met him, he always drove his beloved Camaro.

After making another left turn and driving two

blocks, she eyed the fifties vintage pink and blue neon sign for The Car Dudes. "Nice name."

"They do the best work in town when it comes to classic cars." Mike slowed and steered into the lot. After parking, he opened the door and got out. "I won't be long. Afterward, I'll follow you back to the station."

"Okay." While she waited, Whitney checked her cell phone hoping it would ring then pitched it back into her purse. The sooner they knew what was going on the better. She got out of the car and stretched her legs.

The large beige stucco-sided shop was buzzing with activity. She watched as one of the workers brought Mike's Camaro down off the hoist, and then the two walked into the main building.

A deafening explosion shifted the ground beneath her feet.

A thick wall of heat singed her skin, as small shards of glass became daggers. The impact of the blast jettisoned her and walloped the back of her body into the side of the car. Dazed, she slumped to the ground, gasping, trying to catch her breath from the hard hit to the middle of her back. With her ears ringing, choking gray smoke mixed with the nauseating sweet smell of gasoline. Nausea churned deep in her the pit of her stomach. "Mike!"

Furious orange and blue flames engulfed the bay opening and roared their way up both sides of the building to the roof. Panic struck and a shudder tore through her. She struggled to regain her balance, her feet wobbly and weak, not wanting to cooperate. Eventually able to stand by using the vehicle for support, dizziness assaulted her and she shrunk back to the ground.

She screamed again, her voice barely audible over the thundering flames. "Mike!" Acidity soot touched her tongue and bile crept up her throat. Forcing it down she crawled and watched a man with gray hair scurry out of the garage as flames ate up his blue work pants. He howled like a trapped animal and wailed his arms in the air then patted both legs before finally throwing himself on the ground. He rolled back and forth desperately trying to put out the fire. When he finally did, he sat up, his pants smoldering, his expression frozen with confusion and fear.

Flames shot through the roof and smoke coated the air. Sirens shrieked miles away.

A second blast propelled twisted car parts and wood high into the air and rained down around her like unguided missiles. A piece of metal jetted over her and shattered the back window of a car. Whitney covered her head and ducked. When it was safe she uncovered her head and stiffened half expecting another blast but one didn't come.

Mike stumbled out of the front door opening and fell to his knees. Spotty black soot covered his face, bare arms, and clothing. Behind him, a raging wall of fire popped, crackled and hissed.

Flashing lights cut through the heavy smoke.

She dragged the strap of her shoulder bag and inched her way to him, partially crouching, partially crawling. Her throat tightened. "Help will be here any minute."

He coughed a few times then labored for a breath. "I'm —okay. Are you hurt?"

Minutes later, Whitney watched two fire trucks and an ambulance screech to a stop in the parking lot. "I'm fine. Just a little sore." Her eyes shifted to the other man still perched in the same position, burnt and clearly in shock.

As two EMTs assisted the man and loaded him onto a gurney, another helped Mike to his feet and put an oxygen mask on him. The ambulance attendants slapped the back doors closed, jumped in the vehicle, and rushed out of the lot with the sirens blaring.

Two other ambulances, another fire truck and four police cruisers arrived. As a dozen firemen struggled to get the blaze under control, a male paramedic checked her over. Other than a few bruises and a sore back, she was okay but he wanted to take her to the hospital just in case.

"What about the other man?" Whitney asked.

"He's got third-degree burns on his face, legs, and hands. His condition is grave. Not sure if he's going to make it."

She took a quick sharp breath. Whitney glanced at Mike. Blood trickled from a small gash above his left eye. He pulled down the oxygen mask and stared at the glowing cinders of what was left the garage as if he was mesmerized. He shook his head. "My car is gone, and so are a couple of good friends. Christ, I've known the owner, Jake, for at least a decade."

"I'm sorry about your friends." She could tell he was still in shock. "What happened?"

Another EMT placed the oxygen mask back over Mike's face. "Keep it on. You're suffering from smoke inhalation. We'll be rolling you two out in a few minutes."

Mike narrowed his eyes, not happy having to continue to wear the mask. He waited for the paramedic to walk away before he spoke again. "I don't know what happened in there but the shop didn't go up by its self. It had help. A bomb or something else."

Whitney cringed at his words and her thoughts leapt

to Nathan Shaw.

❊ ❊ ❊

After receiving a call from Whitney, Blake's gut vibrated. His grip tightened around the steering wheel as he sped into the University Medical Center's parking lot. After parking, he jumped out and rushed through the glass revolving door. Panic was thick and swirling. He hated hospitals. Hated the antiseptic smell that came with injuries and illness. Hated seeing others suffering.

With each step, the heels of his boots thudded against the worn gray linoleum floor. Anger forced his hands into fists. He knew the explosion was probably engineered by Nathan Shaw. Who else was the man working with? The blast took direction, preparation and timing. He needed to get the audio surveillance in place at Shaw's house as soon as the sun went down.

He stopped in the hallway and spoke briefly with a thirty-something intern who looked more like a teenager wearing an over-sized white doctor's coat.

"She's fine. No broken bones. Just a few cuts and abrasions. Your friend is okay too. He was treated for smoke inhalation. Both are cleared to leave once I get their discharge orders done. As you can see it's a bit busy in here today." His pager buzzed on his hip. "I have to go."

"Thanks." Blake walked down the wide corridor. He turned right and found Whitney in cubicle ten in the swamped ER. He pulled back the green and orange patterned nylon curtain. Mike was sitting in the chair beside the bed. Black smudges from the smoke dotted his face. Whitney was on the bed with her eyes closed. The navy pantsuit she was wearing was streaked white from ashes. Her eyes popped open and she sat up.

Blake sat on the bed and put his arm around her shoulder, holding her tighter and longer than usual. Her hair and clothing smelled strongly of smoke. "You could have been killed." His tone was harsh and he knew it. He could have lost her like he almost did in Colombia. He glanced at Mike, happy his friend was okay. "You too."

Whitney leaned her head on his shoulder. "We're both fine. We're just a little battered up."

"I spoke with the fire marshal. From their preliminary investigation, the explosion was caused by some type of bomb in or around the area of the Camaro, more than likely triggered by remote. Six people died. The owner, and five employees."

"This is beginning to sound and look more like a cartel move than something Nathan Shaw would dream up himself," Mike added.

Blake had to agree. "I think at this point we have to assume the cartel is involved. Let's hope you're wrong because we just got rid of one problem, or at least we thought we did."

"We were supposed to be safe. History always repeats its self when it comes to Nathan. Remember Andrew West and Pablo Sanchez?"

Blake thought about how Nathan had hired Andrew West to kill him and Whitney. Then there was Pablo Sanchez. Shaw had met the cartel leader while in prison. Together they had hatched a plan to kidnap Whitney, determined to lure Blake to Colombia so Sanchez could kill him—payback for Blake killing Pablo's twin brother over a decade ago. Blake wished he had killed Nathan when he had the chance. He still could.

Whitney swung her legs over the side of the bed. "Why blow up the garage? None of this makes any sense.

If Nathan is pulling the strings, what is he waiting for? Why not just kill us and get it over with?"

"It's part of his game to show he's in control. He gets off on taunting us. We all know Shaw always has a master plan and a carefully organized finale. The finale involves Fielding, and possibly the second scientist in Texas." He kissed her again just as her cell phone rang.

Whitney rooted through her purse and pulled it out. She rose to her feet, her eyes wide and mouthed, "It's Janet Fielding."

Mike looked at him. "I guess her plan worked."

While Whitney went out in the hallway to answer the call, Blake filled Mike in about Shaw's donation to the lab in Texas and about James Nova's untimely death.

"Are the two scientists connected in any other way?"

"Just that they had both worked at BSL-4 labs. We haven't found anything else yet. Did you notice if anyone was following you and Whitney to the garage?

"No one." Mike shook his head. "That asshole owes me a new car and I plan on getting one."

He didn't blame him. Mike loved his car. It had gotten them out of some tight jams over the years including saving their lives on more than a few occasions.

Minutes passed and Whitney returned. She sat down on the edge of the bed. "Janet said four men broke into their house two days ago, and held them at gunpoint. The men said if Matthew Fielding didn't do what they wanted they would kill his wife and their daughter but she didn't know exactly what the men wanted her husband to do because they moved them all into separate rooms. When her husband called at lunch he told her he had done something stupid, something that would change their lives forever." She lowered her voice as a doctor and two nurses walked by. "He said he'd accidentally infected himself with Marburg. He told her he was going to die."

Everyone fell silent.

Blake didn't know much about Marburg other than it was a hemorrhagic fever virus and if you were infected you suffered a horrible and painful death. The men at the warehouse appeared to be homeless by their ragged clothing. All it would take was one person infecting another and things would spiral. The domino effect. A very real and deadly one. "The info Janet Fielding provided is the confirmation we needed. We know for sure Matthew Fielding was infected. The men at the warehouse probably stumbled on his body searching for money or drugs and ended up infecting themselves."

"How many other people did those two men encounter?" Mike asked.

It was a terrifying thought. Blake didn't have the answer.

"Janet said her husband didn't have any physical contact with her or his daughter once he was infected. It killed him knowing he couldn't come home to see them one last time. She also said someone was watching the house and she's convinced her phone line is being monitored. She was happy when she found the cell phone with the flowers because she could call from the backyard where no one could see her."

Blake noticed Whitney fidgeting with the strap of her purse. "We'll get Sofia and Angel on a plane tomorrow and out of Las Vegas with my parents."

Her voice filled with fear. "They have to leave. It's not safe here."

"I want you to go with them."

Her eyebrows raised. "No. That's not happening. I'm

staying here with you."

He smiled, already knowing she wouldn't agree to leave. He figured he'd at least try. The only way Whitney was leaving the country was if he carried her on the plane and handcuffed her to the seat. The thought had crossed his mind. Blake checked his watch. "I want everyone at the house tonight. Mike, if you're feeling up to it, can you give Cally and McBride a call? I'll contact Chambers."

"I'll look after it." Mike stood and fished his cell phone out of the back pocket of his jeans.

Blake turned to Whitney. "Can you ask Jerry to meet us later at the house too? I want to see the footage he took of Fielding's neighborhood. With a bit of luck maybe we'll get an ID on whoever is monitoring the house."

✳ ✳ ✳

Blake jogged through the country club's golf course determined to get the bugs in place at Shaw's house. The sky was clear, and moon's bright glow lit the perfectly manicured fairway guarded by blue water. Hal ran beside him carrying a large black knapsack and his sniper rifle. To the left, a tree-covered hillside sat behind a massive waterfall that fronted the green. Blake spotted two men five-hundred yards away ready to tee-off at the fourth hole next to a small lake surprised to see anyone was on the course. He threw up his hand signaling Hal to stop and shrunk in the shadows of a tree and waited. He spoke quietly into the mic. "We have company."

Hal stopped and crouched. He checked his watch. "It's nine o'clock. I thought the course was closed."

It was supposed to be. "We'll have to sneak past them." He pointed ahead and to the right at several trees perched on top of a two-hundred-foot ledge of rocks. "That's where we need to go. It should lead us directly to the back of Shaw's property."

Hal grinned. "Looks like we have some climbing to do, my friend. We're going to have to make a run for it." Hal shoved the strap of his knapsack back high on his shoulder and expelled a breath. "Ready."

Blake waited until one of the men teed off. "Now." He took off running, legs pumping, glancing over his shoulder every few seconds to make sure the men at the hole hadn't spotted them.

Hal sprinted behind him.

Minutes later, they reached the ridge. After a short break to catch their breath, they started the climb careful not to lose their footing on the treacherous rocks positioned at weird and uneven angles. When they reached the top, Hal set the knapsack on the ground.

It was the perfect entry point. Blake's chest heaved with each breath and hurt, a reminder of where Nathan had shot him years ago. He adjusted his earpiece and mic. "Can you hear me, Cally?"

"Loud and clear."

"We're in position. After Hal takes the shot let me know the moment the ambulance leaves. Make sure no one, no local cops, enter the house. As far as they're concerned, it's the FBI's scene. You're in charge. That should buy us enough time to get the surveillance in place and leave."

"Will do."

Hal handed him the binoculars. "Chamber's isn't going to like this."

Blake couldn't care less what Chambers thought. "I know." He laid on his stomach between two rocks, the fit tighter than he had anticipated. He felt as if he was trapped in an open casket. His heart pounded in his ears as he peered through the night-vision binoculars aimed at the back of Nathan's house.

Lights were on in two of the rooms on the second floor of the house.

"I don't know how you do this." Blake shifted his weight. The edge of a knife sharp rock stabbed into his left thigh. He moved again trying to get comfortable.

"You get used to it. I've been in some tight spots in the past. This one is no different." Hal emptied the knapsack and placed the CheyTac M200.408 bolt-action sniper rifle with a night vision laser scope on the tripod rifle rest. He screwed the suppressor on the end of the barrel to cut down on noise and the muzzle flash. Afterward, he laid flat on his belly and shimmied his body backward on the hard surface until he was in position. "Now we wait."

While they waited, Blake thought about how Shaw had blackmailed them into agreeing to let him see Angel, his words playing over in his mind.

"Imagine what the media will do when they learn the child is the world's first cloned human—that I created her in my lab at ShawBioGen and you and your beautiful bride adopted her, knowing that information. Do you really want that type of chaos in your life? Your honeymoon would be over quite quickly, I would say. Remember, Barnett. I really have nothing to lose by contacting the media. I have nothing to lose, period. I've told you before. You aren't going to win against me."

He shook his head and swallowed a curse. He wanted the man to suffer in any way possible and he was sure Hal would help make that happen. Hal would make sure the shot hurt like hell.

Minutes turned into an hour and Blake was beginning to give up hope they'd see Nathan.

Every muscle in his body throbbed and his elbows were going numb. "There he is." He squinted and watched the man walk to the other end of one of the rooms on the second floor.

"I got him." Hal aligned the scope and placed the crosshairs on Nathan. "Last chance to change your mind. This could all be over."

He wanted to tell Hal to kill Nathan in the worst possible way and it took all his willpower to stop himself from saying, 'kill him'. They needed the man alive, otherwise, they would never know how deep his involvement was in the possible outbreak. "Non-lethal."

Hal took an extra long breath and exhaled.

A few seconds passed.

He fired.

The muzzle flashed and the bullet shrieked into the darkness.

Glass shattered.

Shaw spun sideways, and his body jerked backward, knocking him off balance and into the wall. He didn't know what hit him.

"Target hit. Right forearm."

Blake stared through the binoculars and watched a man run into the same room. He didn't recognize the man. "Shit. There's someone else in the house."

"What do you want me to do?"

If they didn't clear the house they wouldn't get the surveillance in place and possibly lose the chance to learn more about how involved Nathan was with Fielding and the lab. He wiped the moisture that broke out along his hairline and peered into the darkness trying to decide what to do. "Take the shot."

Another flash.

The other man toppled over and hit the floor.

"Target hit. Left calf."

Hal grunted and climbed to his feet. After gathering the spent cartridges and pocketing them he quickly folded the tripod and rest and shoved them into his knapsack.

Blake passed the binoculars to him. "I hope no one else is inside."

"We'll deal with it if we have to. I'm guessing it won't take long before the local cops show up." After closing the bag, Hal heaved the knapsack straps over his one shoulder and swung the leather rifle sling over his other.

Ten minutes went by and sirens roared and grew closer as if riding on the night breeze. Flashing blue and red lights raced up the road. His earpiece crackled followed by a hiss of static.

"I'm not even going to ask why we have two injured instead of one," Cally grumbled.

"You don't want to know. How many local cops are on-scene?"

"Three cars—doubled up. Two ambulances are just pulling in."

"Let me know as soon as they're loaded and ready to leave."

"Roger."

Another ten minutes passed before Blake heard Cally's voice again.

"Both men are in the ambulances." A long pause of silence. "Okay, they're leaving now."

There were six officers on-scene and more would be coming. Blake spoke into his mic. "We're heading in through the back."

"Roger that."

Blake and Hal trudged across the rocks and scrambled over a twelve-foot iron fence. Once they were on the other side, they darted across the lawn, past the swimming pool, and stopped at the glass back door next to the garage.

Blake looked up and spotted a camera pointed toward the driveway. He tried the door handle. "Cally, I need you to shut off the cameras inside and unlock the back door."

"Got it. Give me a few minutes. This place is huge. I have to find the panel."

Minutes later the door opened and Cally appeared. "The cameras are down. Make it quick. Four more locals just arrived. I'm not sure how long I can hold them off. I have to go."

Hal's unshaven face mirrored concern. He dropped the knapsack in a chair with a high wooden back and red velvet gold trimmed seat that looked like it belonged in a palace. He rummaged through the bag and pulled out the listening devices and tools ready to get to work.

Blake knew from experience the local cops would be trying to position themselves as top dog on-scene. It happened more times than he wanted to admit when the FBI was involved. Cally had his work cut out for him. There was no way they would have enough time to search the house before the authorities stormed through the front door. They'd be lucky if they had time to get the surveillance in place and get out. "We need to move fast."

CHAPTER EIGHT

L ater that night the rec-room in their house had been transformed into a mini-command center complete with audio and video equipment, various other pieces of electronic gear, laptops, and monitors.

Whitney gave Angela Donahue a big hug. "It's wonderful to see you again." The woman was stunning with her stylish short black hair and dressed in tight black jeans and a loose army green T-shirt. Whitney was happy Hal had brought her. Angela looked the same as she remembered when she'd helped them get safely out of Colombia after Pablo had kidnapped Whitney.

"Thanks. It's good to see you too. Hal filled me in on what's happening. An outbreak? Scary stuff. I'm glad I can be of help."

"Yeah, it's good to see you, Donahue." Trent Chambers fixed his steely eyes on Blake. "You shot Nathan Shaw? You can't go around shooting whoever you want."

Hal took a couple steps toward Trent. "He didn't. I did."

Blake took a drink of his beer and set the bottle on the coffee table. "It was a judgment call. If it helps keep my family safe and everyone else in this room, then it was justified. We need answers. It was the only way to get

Shaw out of the house, so we could set up surveillance."

"Now you're bugging the guy's house too?"

Hal took another few steps and stopped. "No. I did."

"Have you guys forgotten I'm head of the FBI field office? Your former SAC? How do you figure I'm going to explain this?"

Hal patted Trent on the shoulder as he walked by to get another beer from the bar fridge. "There's nothing to explain."

"For Christ sakes, Hal. I'm surprised you didn't kill him and his butler."

"If I wanted Shaw dead. He'd be dead. You should know that by now."

This was the first Whitney heard about Hal and Blake's escapade. She controlled her expression not to let anyone see her reaction. Blake was keeping secrets from her like he had when they first met, and she wasn't sure she liked it.

"You should have killed him," Blake's father blurted out.

Trent narrowed his eyes at Frank. "You shouldn't even be down here with us. You're not helping matters. No one is killing anyone."

As far as Whitney was concerned, Nathan deserved to die for everything he'd done and for everyone he'd murdered in their lives but considering what they were dealing with now they needed him alive. Nathan was the key to what was going on. His time would come.

Vic Serrano, who used to head the FBI's Cyber Action Team was sitting wearing large black headphones at a make-shift table Blake had constructed by covering the pool table with two pieces of plywood. Now Whitney knew who the man was listening to.

She sat next to Blake on the couch. "We need to get Janet Fielding and her daughter out of their home and somewhere safe before something happens to them."

"I agree," Angela said.

Hal nodded. "Me too. They aren't safe where they are."

"Are we one-hundred percent sure the wife and daughter haven't been infected?" Chambers asked.

The one thing Whitney had learned about Trent over the years he questioned everything. It was part of his job. "Yes, we're sure. I spoke with her and believe her. She's frightened. Her husband was murdered, and the same thing could happen to her and her daughter."

"It's going to be tough getting them out if they're being watched," Chambers said.

"We can do it. Angela and I can go in through the back of the house and grab them," Hal said. "We'll be in and out within minutes."

"Look after it, early before sunrise." Blake turned his attention to Joe Cally and Paul McBride. "I want you guys to make sure my parents and Angel and Sofia board the plane to Aruba tomorrow at one-thirty. Keep your eyes open. There's no telling who's watching."

Whitney touched his shoulder. "I'd feel better if they went with your parents especially after what happened at the garage."

"Are you guys okay with that?" Blake asked.

Joe held up his beer bottle. "Sure. I'm game."

"I'm good with it. It'll be nice to get out of Vegas for a while."

Jerry thumped down the stairs clutching the handle of his camera in one hand. "Sorry, I'm late. I've got something—a guy sitting in a dark gray Chrysler 200 three houses away from the Fielding's house." He set the camera down next to Vic and hit a few buttons. "At first, I thought it was just a resident, but I went back a couple of hours later and he was still there. I did another run by before I came here, and he was gone."

As everyone huddled around the table, Jerry ran the video, fast-forwarding it.

Worry flitted through her mind. "If the man did see Jerry, then Janet and her daughter are in more danger."

Jerry hit the stop button about two minutes in. "That's him. It's not the best shot but it's something."

Whitney gazed at the profile of a man's face with dark brown hair trimmed short around his ears. She didn't recognize him.

Blake continued glaring at the image. "He doesn't look familiar. Not much to go on."

"I did get a shot of the license plate." He pressed the forward button again and stopped thirty seconds later. "There you go."

Blake patted him on the back. "Good job, man. McBride, can you clean up the image, run it, and run the plate?"

"Sure can." McBride opened one of the four laptops and he and Jerry got to work transferring the footage to the laptop.

Trent looked at Hal with a serious look on his face. "You and Angela had better make your move now and go and get Janet Fielding and her daughter. Take them to the safe house in Warm Springs instead of the one on Harmon. Harmon has been comprised too many times by the cartel. And for Christ sakes don't be shooting anyone."

Hal grinned. "I'll try not to. I don't know about Donahue, though."

Trent rolled his eyes not amused by Hal's comments.

"If you see the man in the Chrysler, pick him up." He walked to the corner of the room and started talking with Joe Cally.

After Hal and Angela left, Whitney poured a glass of wine. She was concerned about Janet Fielding and her daughter. Whoever shot her husband probably wouldn't think twice about killing them. Why was Dr. Fielding in the warehouse to begin with? What was he doing there? How did he infect himself with Marburg and who killed him? At least she had evidence to use to confront Dell Summers. She had been right all along. The man had been hiding something during her interview. She heard light footsteps on the stairs and saw Sofia.

The young woman stopped and put her hands on her hips. "I want to stay here with you and Blake. I don't want to go back to Aruba. My father taught me how to do a lot of things. I used to help him at the police station on the weekends. I even went on stakeouts with him. I can help him." She pointed to Vic. "I've done it before."

Blake picked up a set of headphones and handed them to Sofia. "You had better get to work. Ask Vic to fill you in. Write down anything you think is suspicious."

The young woman's eyes glowed and she put on the headphones and sat down next to Vic.

"Thanks for letting her be a part of this. I know it means a lot to her."

"We both know we can't make her get on the plane tomorrow. It'll be good for her and help her deal a little easier with life without Oscar."

Whitney kissed his cheek. "That's why I love you. You're always thinking of others."

His cell phone rang. He tugged the phone from his shirt pocket and checked the display.

An expression ran over his face she couldn't decipher. "What is it?"

"It's a text message from Jason Kurtz." His jaw turned tight and his eyes met hers. "We're supposed to meet at Nathan Shaw's house tomorrow at eleven-thirty with Angel."

Every sound in the room disappeared and everyone stopped what they were doing.

Whitney slumped to the bar stool dazed. Even though she knew the meeting was coming she'd hoped they had a few more days before it was going to happen.

Mike strolled into the room carrying three large pizza boxes, his voice slicing through the silence. "Pizza's here."

Vic removed his headphones and set them on his lap. "We just lost all audio."

Blake shook his head. "The bastard found the bugs. He knows we've been listening."

After a restless night's sleep, Blake yawned and poured Whitney a cup of coffee and one for himself. By the look of the dark shadows under her eyes, she didn't sleep well either. The thought of meeting with Shaw was taking a toll on them. He kissed her cheek and smelled the faint sweet lilac scent of her perfume from last night.

"Hal texted me late last night and said they got Janet Fielding and her daughter to the safe house in Warm Springs without any problems." He sat beside her at the kitchen table and took a sip of his coffee. "Chambers will be debriefing Janet and her daughter personally. He'll call if he learns anything new. Hal said the guy watching Fielding's house wasn't there. He must have gotten spooked."

"At least we know they're safe." She took a drink of her coffee and set the mug down. "Who do you think the man is in Jerry's footage? Do you think he's with the cartel?"

"I think there's a good chance. We can't dismiss anything until we know for sure. I'm hoping to get an ID today, and then we'll know exactly who we are dealing with."

Whitney grasped her mug with both hands and stared at the liquid. "What if Nathan wants to see Angel again after today? What are we going to do?"

"He's not going to. He's seeing her once, and that's it. I'm sick of the bastard controlling our lives."

"If he goes to the media we could lose custody."

He spotted the alarm in the back of her eyes. "I won't let that happen." *I'll kill him myself.*

"Promise me you won't do anything stupid."

Blake heard Angel skipping down the hallway, her thumping footsteps edging closer. "I promise."

The little girl skidded to a stop inside the kitchen doorway. "Cereal please."

"Sure thing, kiddo." Blake went to the cupboard and grabbed the box of cereal and a spoon from the drawer while Angel tugged open the refrigerator and put the carton of milk on the table.

Whitney smiled. "I see you dressed yourself today."

Angel patted her frilly pink blouse and purple pants. Her eyes lit with pride. "These are my special school clothes."

"You look really beautiful, but you won't be going to school today."

The little girl cocked her head to one side. "Why?"

Whitney picked up the child and put her on her lap.

"We have to visit someone and it's really important. It's something we have to do."

Angel frowned. "My teacher said my storybook has to be done."

"I know, sweetie. I'll call your teacher."

Angel shrunk off Whitney's lap and stuck out her bottom lip. "She's going to be mad."

"Don't you worry. She won't be angry with you, I promise." Whitney poured a bowl of cereal with milk and Blake handed Angel a spoon. "If you would like you can watch cartoons while you eat your breakfast."

Angel nodded fiercely. She carefully balanced the bowl with both hands and half walked, half tiptoed out of the kitchen.

"It's killing me we have to take her to see him. I'm worried about how she's going to react. Do you think she will remember him?"

The muscles in his forearms flinched. It was killing him too, more than he was going to admit. He knew it would take all his willpower not to snap Shaw's neck the moment he saw him. "She's a pretty smart kid. She probably remembers everything." He eyed the wall clock above the sink. It was still early. Eight-fifteen. "It will be over within a few hours. Then we'll get her on the plane where she'll be safe with my parents and the guys."

"What about Sofia? Now that's she's staying we need to make sure she's safe at school."

"Already on it. Since McBride and Cally are going to Aruba, she'll have two US marshals with her always. They're parked out front ready to take her to her classes."

"Thank you. You think of everything."

"I'll do anything to protect you and those two girls." He heard a car pull into the driveway. He peered through the kitchen window and spotted Mike heading up the back deck.

The door opened. "Morning. We have an ID on our mystery man from Fielding's neighborhood."

Whitney poured a black coffee and handed it to Mike.

"Thanks." He pulled out a folded piece of paper from his jean's pocket and unfolded it. "The guy's name is Eduardo Diaz."

"Who is he?"

Mike's eyes shifted to Whitney then to Blake. "He used to be one of Pablo Sanchez's personal guards. He used a tourist visa to enter the US last week. Chambers has issued a BOLO though the local cops."

Blake heard Whitney gasp when he mentioned Pablo's name. He set his coffee cup down on the counter harder than he meant to. Warm liquid splashed across his hand. "Shaw is back playing in the cartel's sandbox reconnecting with his old friends. We have two dead scientists, one infected with Marburg, two large donations made by Shaw to both labs where the men worked, and we still don't have any idea what's going on. What's the endgame?"

Whitney stared at him in silence for a long beat then dumped what was left of her coffee down the drain. "Whatever Nathan has planned he's going to make sure he kills all of us."

✳ ✳ ✳

The man peered through the thick glass at the coiled air hoses dangling from the ceiling at different levels, and then to the submarine-style door, the lab's only exit. The newly constructed laboratory was housed in a separate section isolated from the other spaces in the facility. It had its own air and water supply as well as a backup generator in case of a power outage. All the air ducts had been fitted with HEPA filters to catch any airborne organisms. It had taken months to construct the BSL-4 lab two floors below ground level. It was perfectly contained and concealed. No one was aware the lab even existed.

The area looked much like a typical science lab complete with refrigerators, centrifuges, computers, and work hoods. Fluorescent lights glared above, and white paint covered the walls. Everything was in place including the samples of Marburg and smallpox already transported to the site. All that was missing was Dr. Dmitri Cherenkov and his team.

He imagined his contact had paid tens of millions of dollars to have a top Russian scientist working on such a unique project. He was told Cherenkov's father, a Colonel and chief scientist, had helped run the Soviet Union's biological weapons program during the 80's. Dmitri had decided to follow in his father's footsteps, working with some of the world's most lethal pathogens creating biological weapons based on genetically modified agents until he left Russia in 2013 and emigrated to the US. It was scary to think such a man was in this country. For years, the doctor had kept a low profile lending his assistance to foreign countries by offering his expertise and knowledge to the highest bidder. This time Dmitri Cherenkov's job was different. There were no foreign countries to negotiate with and no haggling over prices.

The man walked down the narrow corridor to the locker room and found the scientist and his two male assistants changing out of their street clothes and into surgical scrubs, socks, and underwear.

Dr. Cherenkov was average height, slightly overweight, with a doughy face and manicured nails. He was wearing an expensive chunky gold wristwatch.

The doctor looked up at him as he pulled on a pair of white socks. "Is everything ready for us?"

The man nodded.

"Good." Dmitri turned to his two assistants and motioned his head toward the second room containing the full-body biosafety suits. "As soon as the chimera virus is ready we'll need to test it at least twice and discuss a delivery system. I have a few ideas to meet your needs."

"I'm sure we can find some human subjects for you. My contact did have a small concern. He was worried smallpox may not be as effective as other pathogens, let's say anthrax as an example."

"Tell your contact he has nothing to worry about. Smallpox on its own has about a forty-percent death rate but is highly infectious. By injecting Marburg into the mix, I can genetically mutate both agents to give you exactly what you want. The specific process will allow the new chimera virus to sustain the virulence of smallpox and keep its appearance while looked at under a microscope yet spread a completely different infection. The genetic engineering will be done in bioreactors then we'll process it into an inhalable dust. The particles will also be sealed with plastic to protect them in the air. What your contact will end up with is exactly what he paid for, Resurrect, an extremely effective and deadly virus that will spread like wildfire and kill thousands."

❊ ❊ ❊

Whitney checked her watch for the fourth time and her heart fluttered with dread. She looked out the truck's window at the mammoth house. She did not want to be here. She couldn't believe a killer was living like this. In less than ten minutes they'd be forced to take Angel inside to see Nathan. They should never have been put in this position and Whitney hated it. He should be in prison not free to dictate orders surrounded by veiled threats.

She had no idea how Angel was going to react to seeing him. Her chest was tight with fear. The poor child was nothing more than an experiment born inside his lab and kept there for the first few years only to be known as Angel024. A chill drove up her spine. Angel was Nathan's twenty-fourth attempt to clone a human and his only success, at least as far as they knew. Her thoughts turned to the first time she'd seen the sweet little girl in a video her ex-husband, Mason, had sent her before Nathan had him killed.

A child with long, light-colored hair sat surrounded by toys and stuffed animals.

Someone in a white coat bent and scooped the child from the floor.

"Testing time, Angel. Then chocolate ice cream."

The child let out a tortured screech and flailed her tiny fists, thrashing at the man's face.

"Give me a hand with her, otherwise, I'll be forced to sedate her again."

She felt the warmth of Blake's hand on her knee and she shook the past from her mind. She had to. It was the only way she was going to get through this.

"Are you okay?"

She could see the stress on his face. He was dreading this as much as she was. "I will be." *When it's over.*

There was an uncomfortable silence for a few seconds.

"Can we go?" Angel pointed to the house. "It's big. Does a king live here?"

Whitney wasn't sure if she should laugh or cry by the child's question. There was no way to prepare her for the visit. None. "No. A king doesn't live here. Just a—man."

Blake's gaze shifted to the digital clock on the dash and he opened the door. "Ready?"

Angel joyfully undid her seatbelt and scooted across the seat and into Blake's arms.

The child had no idea what she about to walk into.

He set her on the ground and held her hand.

Whitney opened the door and got out. Apprehension fierce and unrelenting forced her legs to freeze on the spot. She inhaled a deep breath and exhaled. She wasn't going to allow Nathan to do this to her.

Angel grabbed her hand. "Come on. Let's go."

A tall man in his late forties with short brown hair and a well-kept beard greeted them as they walked up the first three steps to the house and ushered them inside.

Walking into the huge circular foyer was like walking into an art museum. Expensive modern art in vibrant shades of blue, red, orange, and yellow cluttered the walls. It certainly wasn't what Whitney envisioned as Nathan's decor choices.

"He'll be with you in a moment."

The man led them into an enormous room filled with an ornate mixture of modern and antique furniture. Her gaze traveled to the wall length built-in bookcase at the far end of the room stuffed with rare leather-bound first editions.

"Please have a seat and make yourself comfortable."

Blake shoved his fists into his pockets. "Thanks. We'll stand. We won't be here long."

"As you wish," the man said, and then exited the room.

Minutes later, Nathan strutted into the living room with a smug look on his face.

Whitney raised her chin and shot him a cool stare. His receding salt and pepper colored hair was clipped short around his ears and his beefy face and beady eyes still reminded her of a stuffed squirrel. Overall, he looked the same, simply older, but just as deadly. His right arm was in a white cast from his hand to above his elbow. The 'wide-eyed weirdo' as Blake always called him was looking her up and down like he always had done in the past and was creeping her out.

"Miss Steel, or should I say, Mrs. Barnett? Congratulations on your marriage. You look as beautiful as ever." His eyes shifted to Blake and the two men played a game of hard-core-stare-down until Nathan spoke again. "This must be the child."

Angel tugged on her hand. "Is his arm hurt?"

Whitney bent and lowered her voice. "I don't know."

"It is hurt. Someone shot me and broke my arm." Nathan narrowed his eyes at Blake for a long moment. "She really does look exactly like your sister. Genetically perfect. I think Claire would be proud. How are you, dear? I'm sure you remember me."

Angel stepped behind Whitney's leg and didn't answer. It was clear she remembered something. Being here was eating Whitney up inside. She felt guilty they'd brought Angel. She wanted to flee but wasn't going to give Nathan the satisfaction of showing her fear, guilt or anything else. They'd be out of here soon.

"Enough with the games," Blake growled. "You saw

her and now we can leave. That's all we agreed to."

"Not so fast. We have much more to talk about including seeing the child again."

Blake laughed. "I don't think so. This is a one-time deal."

Whitney glared at Nathan and straightened her spine. "This isn't happening again."

Nathan smirked. "I don't so. I certainly don't mind contacting the authorities regarding your husband's little shooting expedition last night, and let's not forget these." He pulled out a handful of listening devices from his jacket pocket and flung them on the carpet.

The look on his face chilled her soul.

Blake took a step toward him and stopped. "Typical, Nathan. The only way you can get what you want is by threatening others. I have no idea what you're talking about. I didn't bug your place and if someone shot you I'm one-hundred-percent sure you deserved it. They should have killed you. Maybe the DA's office bugged your place looking to nail your ass again to ensure you go back to where you belong. A prison cell."

"Now who's playing games." Nathan laughed. "It's easy to tell when you're lying. You've never been very good at it. I don't think you're setting a very stellar example for the child, do you?"

"I couldn't care less what you think. How about we talk about Matthew Fielding, Marburg, Eduardo Diaz, and your donations to two BSL-4 labs. We know what you're up to."

Nathan waved his hand as if batting a fly away. "I've donated to many projects and causes over the years. It's not something new. You worked for me. You're fully aware of my incredible generosity. Anything else is your imagination, some story you've concocted."

"I don't believe you. We know you're working with the cartel again. You're going back to your prison buddies. Enjoy your last few days of freedom inside these expensive palace walls while you can."

Angel tugged on Whitney's pant leg and peered at Nathan sideways. "Can we go home? I don't like him."

"I know you don't. Neither do I." She didn't care if she said it out loud or not. "I'm so sorry we had to bring you here. We didn't want to. Remember how I said sometimes we need to do things we don't want to like cleaning your room?"

The little girl frowned and nodded.

"This was one of those times."

Blake gritted his teeth. "Shaw, can't you see you're upsetting her?"

A sly smile tilted the corners of Nathan's mouth. "It's not my intention to upset the child. I only wanted to see her. She is my creation."

Whitney squared her shoulders again. She was sick of the man talking about Angel as if she was an object. "She's not a bloody creation or experiment. She's a little girl. Flesh and blood with a heart and feelings. She doesn't understand why we are here, and neither do I."

Nathan rolled his eyes and picked up a white open box sitting on one of coffee tables. He stepped closer to Angel and stopped. "This is for you, dear. I had this made to look just like you."

How did he know what Angel looked like? He had someone watching them. Panic spiked through Whitney's veins.

Angel cocked her head to one side and blonde curls flopped in her eyes. She glanced at the doll, a spitting image of her. Her face brightened but she made no attempt to take the doll from Nathan.

Whitney grabbed the box from his hands. She felt sorry for the child. They should never have agreed to the meeting and should have taken their chances calling Nathan's bluff. She knew that now as she watched Angel shy away from the man and begin to tremble and sob. "We're leaving."

"I'd like to get to know her. She seems very intelligent for her age."

Blake picked up Angel and held her tight. "Well, she doesn't want to see you."

"She will grow to like me in time. My lawyer will set up another visit."

Nathan's order was hard, emotionless and final.

Blake's jaw tightened. "You're dreaming, Shaw."

As they walked to the front door, Whitney tossed the box on the floor in the foyer, her emotions running hot and wild. "Keep your damn doll."

* * *

After a quick lunch at a home, Blake helped his father carry Angel's suitcases out front of the house and thought about what had happened at Shaw's house earlier. The man had someone monitoring their every move. It was the only way he could have had a doll designed to look identical to Angel. He guessed that person was Eduardo Diaz. The sooner they found him the better. He was baffled as to why Diaz was even involved in Shaw's scheme. He had no personal gain as far as the cartel was concerned. He wasn't even recognized in the cartel ranks unless something had changed in Colombia that Blake didn't know about. It came down to money or revenge for killing Pablo Sanchez. He figured both.

"I really wish Sofia and Whitney could come with us. Your mother is worried sick for their safety and of course for yours as well, especially with what you're dealing with. This is serious. This thing if it's a real outbreak could kill a lot of people."

Blake heard the concern in his father's voice. He leaned against the trunk and instinctively scanned the street. His father was right. If they didn't get a handle on exactly what Shaw was up to they'd be doomed. "I wish they would too, but they are both strong women. Don't worry, they'll be fine. I'll make sure of it."

"It must have been difficult seeing Nathan Shaw. I don't know how you and Whitney did it. After everything he's done I'm shocked he would even have the nerve to even suggest a meeting."

"It was tough on Angel. Tough on all of us. The one thing Shaw has is nerve and he has no fear of any repercussions. He knows he's going back to death row and has nothing to lose. He's a desperate man."

"I still think Hal should have shot him in the head."

Even though Blake agreed with this father, this wasn't Hal's fight. "Believe me, Dad. Shaw will get what's coming to him. You can count on it."

"I'm sure he will. I hope he suffers. We've all suffered enough because of his—actions."

He heard the crack in his father's voice filled with sorrow and loss. It had been tough on his father and mother. Losing Claire had changed their lives forever. He'd watched his parents age ten years in a matter of days following her death. His mother had never been the same. She'd changed from being a vocal woman to being withdrawn, preferring to spend her time alone. He missed his sister every day and would not find any peace until Nathan Shaw was dead. He patted his father on the shoulder. "You can count on it."

Blake spotted Cally and McBride driving down the street toward them in one of the FBI's black SUVs. The vehicle came to a stop behind his father's sedan.

Cally unrolled the passenger window. "Are they ready to go?"

"Yeah." He checked his watch. Almost twelve-thirty. They had an hour before the flight left. "They'll be out in a minute."

Cally gave him a nod and McBride kept the engine idling.

Whitney and his mom walked out the front door of the house with somber looks on their faces. Angel followed wearing a pink and white flowered dress and white sandals. She was clutching her favorite teddy bear. The little girl didn't look thrilled about going away again by the frown on her face. The sight tugged at Blake's heart. The poor kid had spent the first few years of her life living in a lab, and then she was steamrolled into staying in a safe house twice with his parents because of Nathan Shaw and Pablo Sanchez. Then she was sent to foster care until he and Whitney had adopted her. Now she was being shipped off to Aruba for the second time. Many of the same players were involved just different circumstances.

His parents were in their early seventies and it had to be hard on them physically and mentally. Blake hated asking them to help all the time. He knew they didn't mind but it bothered him. All he wanted to do was to give the kid a normal life. So far, he had failed and that didn't sit well with him.

Whitney picked Angel up and gave her a hug. "I love you." She kissed her cheek. "We'll see you soon, okay."

Angel placed her hands on both of Whitney's cheeks and kissed her. "I don't want to go."

"I know you don't. It won't be for long. Only a couple sleep nights."

Blake hoped Whitney was right.

The little girl shrugged. "Two?"

Whitney smiled. "Maybe."

Cally got out of the vehicle and helped his father load the luggage into the back while his mother settled in the backseat.

Whitney passed Angel to Blake.

"I'll see you soon, kiddo. Be good."

Angel's eyebrows raised. "I'm always good."

He gave her a kiss and grinned. "I know you are." He set her in the back seat beside his father, pulled the seatbelt on, and secured it. "We'll see you soon." His eyes shifted to McBride. "Take good care of them."

"You know we will."

Blake closed the door and tapped the roof twice signaling them to leave. He watched the SUV drive away.

"God, this is breaking my heart. How many times do we have to send her away?"

He put his arm around Whitney's shoulder. "This is the last time."

Once inside the house, they headed downstairs to the command center.

Whitney handed him three pieces of paper. "My contact with the police department just emailed me these."

He read the papers; a police report, forensic and autopsy report. The first thing he noticed was the police report wasn't redacted like Fielding's report had been.

"So, the scientist in Texas was murdered and there's no evidence in the autopsy report he was infected with anything."

"My contact followed up with the man's family to make certain. He wasn't sick. Matthew Fielding had accidentally infected himself just like he had told his wife and Dell Summers definitely covered it up."

"We still have two dead scientists whose labs received donations from Shaw. James Nova's murder isn't a consequence. A bit hard to shoot yourself in the head, put the gun back in the glove box and lock it. There wasn't a trace of blood on or near the glove box according to the forensics report."

Whitney nodded. "Nathan needed both scientists for whatever he's planning and used them until he got what he wanted. He had them killed to cover his tracks."

"Sofia will be home from school soon." He pulled a gun out from the back of his jeans and handed it to her. "I want you carrying this all the time. Take it everywhere you go."

She took the weapon and gripped the handle. "A Ruger LC9 with an aftermarket grip."

Blake grinned always astonished by his wife's weapons know-how. "That's why I love you. You're a woman who knows her guns."

"Thank my father. He taught me everything I know."

She went silent. It was difficult losing her father in Colombia and losing her mother to a drunk driver. Even though Blake believed Alejandro Quintero had been playing games when he'd told Whitney she looked like her father and acted as if the man was alive, there was no proof whatsoever the man was alive. For Whitney's sake, he would continue to ask around and keep on his contacts in Colombia until she had the answers she needed.

"Where do you want to go from here?"

"I'm going back to the station and contacting the CDC again and Dell Summers. This is his chance to come clean because Travis wants an update and I know my boss well. He's going to want me to go live with what we have so far."

Blake rubbed the back of his neck and thought for a few seconds. "It might be a good thing, going live. It'll send a clear message to Shaw and everyone else involved that we're on to them."

"It could. It could also create panic and fear. Remember the last Ebola outbreak?"

He remembered it well. Panic had shut down schools and certain airports. Some countries had closed their borders due to fear. The outbreak also prompted docks in Mexico and Belize to refuse a cruise ship because a healthcare worker on board had helped care for a man who'd died from Ebola even though the worker never had any direct contact with the man.

"Going live will put you in danger."

"I'm already in danger. We all are. Reporting the story isn't going to change that. We'll only be safe when we stop whatever Nathan has planned and he's dead."

The woman had a point. "If you plan on going through with this I'll call Chambers right now. Homeland Security, the CIA and NSA need to be involved in case we have a panic outbreak."

CHAPTER NINE

"You're late." The man loosened his tie. He stared at his friend who was almost six-foot-tall with brown hair buzzed short against his skull. His bare arms were etched with scars that told a story, one of hardship and survival.

"It couldn't be helped. It took a lot longer than expected. They've moved the scientist's wife and daughter to a house in Warm Springs. It appears to be some type of a safe house."

"Interesting." The man thought for a long moment. "It doesn't matter. They don't know anything."

"There is something else. I think the reporter knows who I am. I saw a man driving up and down the scientist's street. The reporter was there at Fielding's house dropping off flowers to his wife. It looked like the man driving around was filming the area. I'm sure he saw me. Not that anyone can connect me to the scientist or his family. As far as anyone is concerned I'm in the country on vacation."

"That certainly makes things a wee bit more difficult." He hesitated. "But certainly, not impossible."

"How much longer until the virus is ready?"

The man watched Dr. Cherenkov and his assistants through the glass and wondered what type of a person could work under such perilous conditions. One mistake, one small hole in your suit could cost you your life. It would require a certain type of temperament. He also knew the biosafety suits were extremely cumbersome, weighing ten pounds, and adding six inches of height making the doctor and his team look like giant marshmallow men. "They're finishing up now. He wants to test the virus before he dries the particles. Were you able to get what I asked for?"

His friend nodded. "I have three homeless men."

"Excellent. They will be the perfect subjects. No one will miss them."

"It was quite easy convincing them to come with me. I gave them each a one-hundred-dollar bill and promised another hundred when they were done."

The chosen vagabonds didn't know they weren't leaving, at least not alive. The man glanced at his friend then back to Dr. Cherenkov who gave him a nod indicating the completion of the first stage. "I'm excited to see how the virus works but first I'd like to meet our fine test subjects. Then you need to change your appearance, so we don't have the authorities breathing down our necks."

* * *

Travis sat across from Whitney's desk, his eyelids

heavy. "I agree. Give the CDC and Dell Summers one last chance to comment. If they don't, go live this afternoon with what you have. The public deserves to know about Dr. Fielding and that he was infected with Marburg. There may be other people out there who came into contact with him and aren't aware they've been infected."

"And unknowingly spreading the infection to others." Her boss looked tired and she wondered what was going on with him. He'd been away from the station a lot lately. She spent the next few minutes filling him in on what she knew.

"Stick to the facts about Nathan Shaw since there isn't any proof of his involvement other than the donations. At this point, the station doesn't need a lawsuit."

Whitney was happy he was on board with her plan. He usually was no matter the topic. "Is everything okay? You really look beat today."

"I'm fine. Just dealing with some family issues."

She knew he'd remarried last year and was having problems with his stepson who'd been arrested for dealing drugs in one of the casinos two months ago. "I'm sorry. I'm sure everything will work out."

"It will, but I won't be around much over the next week. I'm sure you and Jerry can hold down the fort." He cleared his throat and stood. "I need to go. I've got another appointment. Keep me updated."

After Travis left, Whitney dialed the CDC's number and waited on hold.

She already missed Angel. It was going to be hard not having her around, but she knew the little girl would be out of harm's way safe with Blake's parents, Cally and McBride. She'd be safe in Aruba far away from Nathan Shaw.

The director's secretary came on the line and Whitney told the woman why she was calling.

"This is Whitney Steel. I was hoping to speak to the director regarding Dr. Matthew Fielding.

"I'm sorry. Director Greeden has no comment."

"I know Dr. Fielding and two other men were infected with Marburg. Have the two men died as well? The public has the right to know. It's the CDC's job to inform the public of an outbreak."

A long beat of silence.

"I'm sure you are fully aware the law allows the withholding of information from the public when certain incidents involve specific safeguard and security measures."

It was apparent the woman was citing directly from the 2002 law. "I'm fully aware Marburg is on the federal list of special agents and toxins as a potential bioterror pathogen. Doesn't a single case of a communicable disease not previously recognized in an area constitute an outbreak? Shouldn't it be reported, investigated and relayed to the public? We're talking about public safety here."

"Again, Miss Steel. Director Greeden has no comment at this time. Have a nice day."

Whitney heard a click on the other end of the phone.

She shook her head not feeling too confident about the CDC. They weren't only a lab operator, they co-ran the Federal Select Agent Program that regulated and inspected military, university, and private labs working with regulated bacteria, toxins and viruses. The CDC was one of a tiny group of biolab operators with the some of the worst regulatory track records in the US after receiving numerous sanctions under federal regulations for mishandling bioterror germs.

If the director thought Whitney would keep her mouth shut, he was wrong. She was a reporter and the public had the right to know what was going on.

Next Whitney called Flatiron Sargasso Laboratories and asked to speak with Dell Summers. His secretary put her through immediately.

"Whitney, how can I help you?"

"I have a few more questions and I wanted to speak to you before I go live later today."

"I'd be glad to answer them if I can."

"Can you tell me more about the cash donation Nathan Shaw made to your lab? Was it for a specific project?"

"I'm sorry I can't speak about private donations made to Flatiron Sargasso or specific research projects."

She heard Jerry talking to Mike in the hallway outside her office.

"I understand, Mr. Summers. The reason I'm asking is because Mr. Shaw was in prison when he made the donation. It doesn't seem morally right that a man who was sentenced to death was making large cash donations to anything let alone two BSL-4 labs, not just yours, but also one in Texas. I thought you might want to comment on the subject."

"I am unable to comment on any private donations or anything about our contributors due to confidentiality."

"The information you aren't willing to share with me is mostly public knowledge. All it takes is a quick Internet search." She waited a few seconds to see if he would answer.

"It doesn't mean I can personally talk about them. What exactly do you want from me?"

The soft tone of his voice changed to impatience with a touch of anger around the edges. Whitney knew she'd struck a chord with the man.

"I want answers. Dr. Fielding was infected with Marburg while working in your lab and you and the CDC are covering it up. Was the incident reported? Are any other samples missing? What exactly happened to Dr. Fielding? This is your chance to tell your side of the story before I go live."

"I have nothing more to say." He hung up.

Whitney put down the receiver. She wasn't shocked at all by the brush-off twice in one day. One thing she'd learned as a reporter, innocent people love to talk. Guilty ones when they are caught red-handed, not so much. Out of fairness to Blake's secretary, she made a mental note to contact Michelle to let her know she was going to report details about her uncle's death the woman probably hadn't heard about yet.

Jerry poked his head inside the door. "So, what's the verdict?"

"Get everything ready. We're going live outside Flatiron Sargasso in an hour."

"I want to personally thank each of you for participating. What we learn from you today will help us immensely." The man looked each of the test subjects over. The three men looked and smelled as if they hadn't taken a bath in months. The nasty smell of urine, body odor, and feces sat heavy in the air. The stench was rancid and almost made him gag.

The man with no teeth grimaced. "Will it take long?"

"Not at all. You'll each be given an injection of the—

vitamin and we'll observe you for a few hours."

No-teeth eyed him suspiciously. "Why you gotta watch us?"

"Just in case you are allergic to the injection. Some people have allergies to certain things."

The shortest man of the group with a scar over his left eye viciously scratched his arm as if he was infested with bugs. "Will you feed us? I'm hungry."

"We certainly don't want you to go hungry. We'll have some food brought to you immediately."

He felt a flicker of guilt for what they were about to do but these men would be much better off where they were going than living on the streets.

"Can we smoke?" The twenty-something male with long greasy hair pulled out a crumpled pack of cigarettes from his tattered shirt pocket.

"Yes." He'd give the man the name, Smoker. He didn't know their real names and didn't want to.

"How 'bout a bottle of whiskey. We ain't picky."

"I'll see what I can do."

A murmur of excitement permeated the room along with the foul air. The homeless men grinned at each other as if they had hit the jackpot.

He cleared his throat to get their attention. "The doctor will be in soon and give you the injection. The man walked to the door. "We'll be back in a little while. Thank you again."

After he left the room and locked the door, he looked at Eduardo. "Dr. Cherenkov will be giving them a short-acting sedative. Once they're out we'll move them into the isolation lab where he'll inject them with the virus."

"Are we going to feed them first?"

"I'm not completely cold-hearted. There are two

pizzas and some wine in the kitchen. The men are hungry. They might as well enjoy their last meal."

While Eduardo went to get the food for the men, the man met Dr. Cherenkov in the hallway.

"Are my test subjects ready?"

"We'll give them thirty minutes or so to eat. It doesn't look as if they've eaten for days. It's the least we can do considering what we're about to do."

"This is your show. Whatever you would like. I'll be in the kitchen having a coffee. Let me know when they're ready."

The man nodded and watched the doctor walk away. His cell phone beeped. He grasped the phone from his suit jacket pocket. "Hello."

"It's Dell Summers. Whitney Steel knows about Fielding being infected with Marburg. She's going to do a live report this afternoon. She said I'm covering up everything. This wasn't supposed to happen. You promised me I'd be safe if I helped. If she goes public the regulators are going to know a specimen is missing and wasn't reported."

This was the last thing they needed especially when they were so close. The woman was smart. Too smart. His contact had warned him numerous times. He should have listened.

"Report the missing specimen right now. As far as anyone is concerned you didn't know it was missing until the inventory was re-checked. Tell whatever story you need to. I'll call you back in ten minutes. Get it done." He disconnected the call, hit speed dial, and waited for his contact to answer.

"What is it?"

"We have a problem." He quickly told his contact the

details.

"She's a highly intelligent woman. Have Eduardo look after it."

He hadn't told his contact about the BOLO issued for his friend and wasn't going to. Eduardo had his own men in place to help out if needed. "You want her killed?"

There was a short hiss on the other end.

"She's going to report the story regardless, but it does appear the woman requires a small surprise, something that will make her think twice to back away. Do not kill her. Find a way to scare her enough to buy a few more days. I'd much rather wait until the virus is ready, so I can watch her and her husband suffer an agonizingly painful death."

By late afternoon dark slate-colored clouds raced by warning of an imminent storm. A warm desert wind kicked up and blew dust from the street straight into Whitney's face. She squinted and pushed her hair out of her eyes. Traffic on the street was steady as if drivers were trying to rush home before the rain. Every now and then, a driver would honk and wave. Reporting live in front of Flatiron Sargasso Laboratories was perfect especially after her conversation with Dell Summers. The man had lied and knew much more than he was willing to reveal. On the other side of the fence, she watched as one of the facility's white security vehicles was making its rounds. They were fully aware she was here and were keeping an eye on her.

While Mike and Blake helped Jerry, finish setting up the equipment she paced, clutching the microphone in her right hand and went over in her head what she was going to say.

"Mike and I will be over there." Blake pointed to the corner of the gate.

She was happy they were both here. After the explosion at the garage, everyone was on high alert. No one was taking any risks.

"I doubt anyone involved would make a bold move right here with so much security on the other side of the fence. I'm more concerned if my report is going to create panic. We've seen it happen before."

"Let's hope not." He pushed her a strand of hair out of her face. "You're doing the right thing. Everyone needs to know."

It was the right thing to do. It was her job. Whitney smiled, wishing she didn't have such a horrible feeling of nervousness in her stomach.

"I'm ready," Jerry said.

Whitney nodded.

Jerry held up his fingers for the countdown. "In five... four...three...two...one."

She drew a deep breath and exhaled. The red light on the camera flicked on indicating they were on-air. "I'm reporting live outside Flatiron Sargasso on West Charleston Boulevard where Dr. Matthew Fielding, a senior scientist at the facility was found in an abandoned warehouse dead from an apparent gunshot wound to his head. More disturbing is the fact Dr. Fielding was infected with Marburg at this very lab."

"In an interview, Dell Summers, Flatiron Sargasso's Director of Science, stated there were no incidents at the lab or any pathogen inventory discrepancies. When asked again earlier today, he said he had nothing more to say."

"Marburg, a form of viral hemorrhagic fever is transmitted by direct contact with blood, body fluids and tissue of an infected person. The virus is fatal in seventy-five percent of all cases and is among one of the most virulent pathogens known to infect humans. Symptoms begin suddenly, with an intense headache and malaise followed by haemorrhagic manifestations usually between days five and seven. Most fatal cases develop bleeding from multiple sites."

"Along with Dr. Fielding, two homeless men who discovered his body were also infected. The men and Dr. Fielding were taken away by the CDC's Rapid Response Team to an undisclosed location. The condition of the homeless men is not known, or if any of the three men had contact with others and spread the virus. News3 has contacted the CDC numerous times. Director Don Greeden's office stated he has no comment."

"News3 has also learned Nathan Shaw made a multi-million-dollar donation to Flatiron Sargasso while incarcerated at Carson State Prison. He also donated millions of dollars to another lab, Genomics BioMedical in San Antonio, Texas where a scientist by the name of James Nova was murdered the day before the body of Dr. Fielding was discovered here in Las Vegas.

Fat raindrops splattered against her bare arms and sent a chill through her body.

"Mr. Shaw until recently was on death row for hiring a hitman to kill Claire Barnett, a microbiologist with his company, ShawBioGen, and for his involvement in the murders of Senator Mason Bailey, George Raines, an editor with WBNN-TV, and Las Vegas District Attorney Kate Leathham in hopes of covering up his illegal human cloning project. He was released on twenty-million-dollars bail and is under house arrest after his lawyer, Warren Demotteo, convinced the Nevada Supreme Court that his client wasn't provided adequate representation. The retrial will take place—"

Tires squawked.

An alarm sounded in Whitney's head and her spine tingled. Her head snapped to the right.

A black Ford Escape with tinted windows slowed. The driver's window lowered.

She spotted the barrel of a gun.

Mike and Blake yelled in unison, "Get down!"

Fear swept through her. Whitney dropped the microphone and dove to the ground.

A shot rang out.

The slug hit one of the rails of the metal gate with a loud clang and ricocheted back toward the street.

Her fingers clawed, trying to grasp the handle of the Ruger LC9 inside her shoulder bag. She yanked out the gun and rolled on her side, positioning herself to take a shot. Her heartbeat pounded in her ears and adrenaline prickled. She fired twice in rapid succession. Both shots torpedoed into the passenger rear door. She wrenched her eyes to Jerry. He sprinted in front of her, feet thudding, balancing the camera on his shoulder and leapt for cover behind an enormous cactus.

The driver fired again. And again.

A bullet whizzed past her left shoulder and burrowed into the ground, spraying a small explosion of clay around her. The rain sharpened, and the smell of the earth left a gritty taste in her mouth. She had no idea where the second shot struck but from her vantage point, it appeared everyone was safe.

Horns blared.

Blake and Mike fired their weapons.

A slew of bullets drilled into the rear panel of the vehicle as traffic screeched to a stop in both directions.

The driver gunned the engine. The Escape swerved into the outside lane and accelerated past the vehicles stopped in the middle of the street.

An older BMW screeched to a stop.

Whitney's heart raced. She bounced to her feet, and squeezed off another round, taking out one of the taillights as the vehicle sped away.

Blake and Mike bolted, zig-zagging through the traffic to Blake's truck, jumped in, and sped after the driver, tires smoking.

She lowered the gun to her side. Slivers of rain slashed at her cheeks. Her black pants and turquoise top were dirty and drenched from the rain. She sucked in a deep breath and let it out trying to calm herself and slow her racing heart. She realized Jerry had probably been on-air the whole time. She slung the strap of her purse over her shoulder and walked toward the cactus. "It's okay now. You can come out." When Jerry didn't answer, goosebumps erupted over her arms and legs. She quickened her pace.

Her heartbeat leapt and the gun slipped out of her hand.

Oh God no.

She dropped to her knees and knelt next to him.

He was sitting, slumped over. Blood gushed from the left side of his chest and fanned out across his shirt, soaking the waistband of his tan pants.

She quickly shrugged off her jacket and pressed it against the wound and took his hand and told him to hold it there.

Sirens howled and grew louder by the second.

A gurgling sound echoed from his chest. His mouth moved but no speech came out. He kept trying to speak, his jaw working hard with no success.

"Don't try to talk." Rain bit at her face and she feverishly dug through her purse for her cell phone and dialed 911.

Each breath turned into a struggle.

"Hold on, Jerry. Please."

His eyes widened and had an odd look in them, an eerie blankness. Whitney held his hand tight.

She couldn't lose him too. She'd lost enough, too many people she cared about.

His chest rose one last time.

And tears streamed down Whitney's cheeks.

CHAPTER TEN

T he man watched through the large window in the door as Dr. Cherenkov injected the last man with the short-acting anesthetic. Within minutes, the men were sound asleep. From what the doctor had told him, the men would be out for about fifteen minutes, giving them just enough time to do what they needed to do.

"The reporter issue has been dealt with by one of my men. I'm sure she will back off now. I was told her cameraman was killed."

He didn't care to hear the details as long as the job was done to his contact's satisfaction. Slowing the woman down was their number one goal. The man glanced at Eduardo pleased he had altered his appearance. His dark brown hair was now blond, almost white, and he wore thick-framed black glasses. No one would recognize him not even the authorities. "Good work."

Eduardo nodded. "Were they happy with their meal?"

"Yes. Very much so. They wanted to stay here longer than originally agreed to. Who would have thought?"

When Dr. Cherenkov was done, he left the room and stripped off his white lab coat and blue latex gloves. "You'd better get them moved while I get suited up. We don't have much time before they wake up."

The man turned to his friend. "I'll need your help."

Eduardo nodded again. "I'll get the gurneys."

"How long before the men are symptomatic?" The man asked.

"The normal incubation times for Marburg and small-pox is anywhere from 5-14 days. During this time, they wouldn't be contagious."

The doctor's bushy eyebrows lifted as he spoke, and he had a gleam in his eyes. He was excited to see the results of Resurrect.

"Because we've genetically modified both pathogens and made it into one virus symptoms will appear almost immediately and will be much more severe. It begins with the usual symptoms of most infectious diseases. A headache, chills, fever, body aches and vomiting. Next, comes the rashes, sores filled with fluid, delirium, shock, liver failure, massive hemorrhaging from the ears, mouth, and eyes, and then multi-organ shutdown. I can predict with extreme confidence the men will be dead within three to four hours."

Once the men were transferred to the isolation unit, the man waited for Dr. Cherenko to put on his biosafety suit. He wasn't sure what to expect once the subjects were injected with the chimera virus, but he knew by the doctor's horrifying details of the symptoms the homeless men were going to die an atrocious gruesome death. At least it would be quick, and they wouldn't suffer for long. God rest their souls.

Ten minutes passed, and the doctor returned.

"It's done. Now we wait and observe. My assistants are in the lab sealing the particles, so we can do the final test on a larger scale tomorrow."

* * *

Sirens were all around Whitney, shrieking, echoing in her head. All she wanted was peace and quiet, so she could try to banish the images of Jerry dying. She had no idea how long she'd been sitting with her legs drawn up to her chest oblivious to the commotion going on around her. The world tilted and swayed. She closed her eyes for a brief minute. Another loss. Another person dead in her life.

Whitney opened her eyes. Blake held out a hand and helped her to her feet while the paramedics loaded Jerry's body into the back of the ambulance.

Tears welled up in her eyes. Her heart hurt, and all-too-familiar guilt twisted inside her.

He slipped his arms around her and hugged her close. "I'm sorry. Jerry was a good guy."

"Jerry was a kind man and a good friend. He didn't deserve to die. This should never have happened. Did you get the driver?"

"No. But we have the plate number."

She looked him in the eye and knew he didn't have all the answers. She needed some. "That's not enough. I want the man who did this. He killed Jerry. It's like reliving the past over and over. Mason, George—your sister. So much death. It had to be Eduardo or someone else Nathan had paid off. When is this going to end?"

He hugged her again, then released her. "I know. We'll find him. Mike and Chambers are dealing with the cops. We're free to leave."

As they walked together through the thickening police presence crime scene techs were busy working the area. She glanced over her shoulder at Flatiron Sargasso Laboratories.

Dell Summers was the only person who knew she was

going to be reporting live.

Her entire body stilled.

She wanted to kill Nathan.

She knew with every fiber of her being he was the one sitting back giving the orders like he always did. Whitney was going make sure he paid for everyone he'd taken in her life.

* * *

A blood-stained hand smacked against the glass divider safely separating the man from No-teeth on the other side. The man flinched and took a step back shocked by what he was witnessing.

Blood streamed from the homeless man's nose, ears, corners of his eyes, and the whites of his eyes had been transformed into a vivid shade of yellow. Sweat dripped off his scruffy unshaven chin and mixed with blood, soaking the collar of his shirt.

"Help—me." No-teeth pounded his fist against the glass, barely able to stand, his body violently shaking from the high fever.

"Not in my wildest dreams could I have predicted such success of the chimera virus." Dr. Cherenkov glanced at his watch. "The men already have massive hemorrhaging from multiple spots within one hour of injecting the virus."

"Help—me—you—fucker!" No-teeth yelled a flurry of curses followed by an ear-piercing scream. Blood splattered against the glass.

The doctor ignored the man's pleas. "Notice the red spots on his tongue and all the small sores filled with thick, opaque fluid on his skin? Smallpox. I would never have thought the virus would have worked this quickly."

No-teeth raised a shaky fist ready to pound the glass again but collapsed to the floor and rolled onto his side

In the corner of the room, the Smoker sat hugging his knees, his muscles jerking, gnawing on his bottom lip with yellow nicotine-stained teeth like a squirrel with a nut. The third test subject was sprawled out on one of the beds vomiting all over himself, too weak to hit the pail next to the bed.

His throat thickened. He felt as if he was in the middle of a horror movie. It was probably a good thing the virus was working much faster than the doctor had anticipated. The men wouldn't have to suffer any longer than necessary for Dr. Cherenkov to gather the data he needed to guarantee Resurrect was doing what it was supposed to do. From what the man was seeing, he'd say the test was successful.

"My assistants will be going in to take blood and tissue samples. At this point, the men are far too frail and sick to care. They will be grateful for the human contact. It will be their last."

"Once you get what you need will you give them something to put them out of their misery?"

"We will. Not until after the first man dies. It's important to document exactly how long it takes from when the virus was injected to symptom onset to death."

By the way, No-teeth looked, he probably wouldn't be alive much longer. The man observed the assistants entering the room. The Smoker twisted his head acknowledging their presence then projectile crimson colored vomit splatted against the two assistant's biosafety suits. The man in the corner was now flat on his back on the floor thrashing about. He abruptly stopped moving. It was hard to tell if he was still breathing.

After the necessary samples were taken from the first two men, No-teeth lost control of his bladder and a puddle formed beside his leg and mixed with blood. He slithered his body like a slow-moving snake across the floor toward them. He reached into his pocket and pulled out something.

"What is he doing?"

Dr. Cherenkov raised an eyebrow. "I don't know. I'm shocked he has any strength to move."

The man spotted the glint of a blade. "Shit. He's got a knife!"

With a sharp curse, the doctor clobbered his palm against the intercom button on the wall. "Get out of there!"

The one assistant peered through his clear visor and had a confused look on his face. He turned, ready to follow the other assistant out of the room to the decontamination showers.

No-teeth stabbed himself in the chest with fury then wildly slashed at the assistant's suit over and over. He dropped the knife and the side of his face hit the floor with a crack. He was either unconscious or dead.

The man shook his head in disbelief by No-teeth's speed. It was if the man had gotten a sudden end of life jolt of energy.

The assistant spun as quickly as he could in the bulky suit, his eyes huge and round when he realized what had happened. He looked down at the shredded leg of the rubber suit at the small puncture wound in his calf. He slowly lifted his head.

"You know you can't leave, Aleksei," Dr. Cherenkov said. "I'm sorry."

"I know." His voice filled with panic. "I—I need to call

my family before..."

"I'll bring a cell phone in for you in a little while. I'll make sure you're as comfortable as possible. I won't allow you to suffer."

"Thank you, Demitri. It has been an honor working with you for the past five years."

Dr. Cherenkov removed his hand from the intercom button and was silent.

"I'm sorry about your friend."

"It happens." The doctor frowned. "Aleksei is a brilliant young scientist. It's such a shame. However, he's aware of the risks every time he puts on a suit." He paused for a few seconds. "Have you chosen a site for the second test? I would suggest a place that is intimate and crowded."

The man forced himself to think. "I have the perfect spot. The Four Spades is a medium-sized slot room. Lots of action. It's located behind the Flamingo Casino."

"I'll need the floor and ventilation system plans so I can choose the best delivery method."

"What are our options for the big event?"

"There are various options. It could be delivered by explosive bomblet, diffusing the agent as an aerosol. By using this method, the virus could be dispersed over a wide area. Using an agent generator, which is a pressurized container while in flight doesn't kill as many of the particles as an explosive bomblet. Another method would be using spray tanks while on a plane. It uses a pressurized form and a nozzle device to aerosol the virus. The loss of agent is about the same as using a generator. Lastly, would be to use a missile warhead, which would disperse in a circle pattern. We don't have a missile sitting around so I would suggest one of the other methods."

"I'll have Eduardo get whatever you need."

* * *

"Is Whitney okay?" Sofia asked. "She's been in the bedroom for almost two hours."

Blake dried the last plate and put it in the cupboard. He glanced out the kitchen window at the quarter moon poking through the clouds. "She just needs some time to herself. She's really upset about Jerry."

"I saved her some Bandeja Paisa. It's in the fridge when she feels up to eating. I know it's her favorite."

"Thanks. I know she'll appreciate it. How are you doing through everything?"

"I'm—okay."

He heard the uncertainty in her voice. "Are you sure?"

Her eyes flashed with fear for a split second.

She shook her head. "I'm scared."

He set the tea towel on the counter. "I know. We're all scared."

She shot him a look of surprise. "Even you?"

"It's hard not to be under the circumstances. Jerry being killed, and an outbreak of Marburg is as serious as it gets. Are you regretting not going with Angel and my parents back to Aruba?"

"A bit. I miss Angel. She's like my kid sister."

"Yeah, I miss her too. It sure is awfully quiet around here." He opened the fridge and pulled out a beer. After opening it he took a long drink and set the bottle next to the sink. "I think it would be a good idea if you went to the safe house in Warm Springs. Matthew Fielding's wife is there with her daughter. She's the same age as you. It's your choice."

Sofia hated to miss school, but he'd feel a lot better if she went to the safe house until they had some type of confirmation as to how many people were infected and where.

Sofia let the plug out of the sink and watched the soapy water go down the drain. "Okay. I'll go."

"I'll have Angela Donahue come and get you. You'll be safe there." His cell phone rang. "One sec." He grabbed the phone off the kitchen table, checked the display, and noticed it was Mike calling. "What do you have?"

"The state troopers found the SUV abandoned on the side of the road about twenty miles north outside of Las Vegas on Interstate 15. It was reported stolen early this morning. The owner lives on the same block as Fielding."

"Any prints?"

"A couple. The locals are running them right now."

"Good. I doubt Diaz would risk being seen in public with a BOLO out for him. The prints probably belong to the owner of the SUV or one of Eduardo's men."

The *Sur de Calle* cartel had a large network of soldiers in the US ready to step up to help Eduardo out. Smuggling drugs and guns into the country was a multi-billion-dollar business and took a lot of manpower to ensure things ran smoothly.

"You're probably right. We should have something soon. How's Whitney?"

"She's still upset. It was the last thing any of us thought would happen today. Keep me posted."

"Will do." He disconnected the call and spotted Whitney heading toward the kitchen. Her eyes were puffy and red. Losing Jerry had hit her hard.

Sofia flipped her hair over her shoulder and dried her hands with the towel. "I think I'd better go and get packed."

Whitney stood in the doorway and watched the young woman leave the room. "Did I miss something?"

"I was able to convince her to go the safe house in Warm Springs."

"I'm glad she agreed." She pulled out a chair and sat at the table.

Blake opened the fridge and grabbed the plate of food Sofia had made and put the meal in the microwave to heat. "Me too. She's scared."

"I can't believe Jerry is dead. Dell Summers is the only person who knew I was going to do the report."

"It's pretty obvious by everything that's happened Shaw is the ringleader. He always is."

She leaned her elbows on the table and looked up at him. "What are we going to do? People are dying, and we don't know what he has planned. Why kill Jerry? He has nothing to do with any of this."

"First thing's first." After grabbing a knife and fork Blake opened the microwave and set the plate of food and cutlery on the table in front of her. "You need to eat." He poured her a glass of wine.

She gave him a small smile and took a drink. "Thanks."

"Jerry got caught in the crossfire. I don't believe he was the target. He was there with you doing his job."

"I was the target because of my report calling out Nathan and Dell Summers."

A tic pulsed in his jaw and she could almost feel the anger brewing inside him because she was feeling the same thing.

"Definitely. It was a warning just like the garage explosion. Shaw's shaking in his boots, worried we're getting close to discovering what game he's playing this time around."

Her shoulders slumped. "If I hadn't done the report, Jerry would still be alive."

He felt helpless unable to find a way to comfort her. He knew guilt wasn't satisfied with explanations though it still needed to be said. "What happened isn't your fault. The only people to blame are the shooter and Shaw."

She took a few mouthfuls of the beef and rice dish and set the fork down on the edge of the plate. "I'm still trying to figure out why Matthew Fielding was in the warehouse. The men who held him and his family at gunpoint told him to follow their exact orders. What were their orders? What was he doing there?"

"I don't know." He shook his head. "Why was he in the warehouse when he knew he was infected with Marburg? I think I should have a chat with Summers first thing in the morning. He seems to be one of the major players together with Shaw and Eduardo Diaz."

She shrugged. "I wish we knew."

Awkward silence took over the kitchen and for the first time, Blake was lost for words unable to put all the puzzle pieces together.

"I want Nathan out of our lives now before he kills you, Sofia or Angel."

There was a harshness in her voice Blake had never heard before and it worried him. "So do I." He didn't want to say the words, but it was the truth. They needed the Shaw alive. "Until we figure out what his endgame is we're stuck with him. After that—anything goes."

Three loud dings came from Whitney's cell phone. He passed her purse across the table knowing she was waiting to hear from her boss with Jerry's sister's contact information, so they could send their condolences.

After retrieving the phone, she read the message.

"Two biological agents. Chimera virus. It's a genie no one wants let out of a bottle."

She looked up at him with wide eyes and handed him the phone. "You need to read this."

Blake read the screen. His chest tightened. "Christ. We're not just dealing with one pathogen."

Blake knew a chimera virus was created by using two or more different agents. Biological warfare was one of the largest threats the world was facing and had been for decades.

She pushed the plate of food to the side of the table and bit her bottom lip. "We have to find out what James Nova was working with at his lab. Now we know why Matthew Fielding was in the warehouse. He was delivering a sample of Marburg—"

"To Eduardo."

She bit her bottom lip. "Dell Summers is on Nathan's payroll. From what I've read Marburg is listed as a category A biowarfare agent under the CDC's classification system."

He stared at the email address and uneasiness crept through his body. "Do you know who sent the message?"

She shook her head. "The address isn't familiar and it's not on any of my contact lists."

"Maybe Summers sent it since he knows you're on to him. Or Shaw is playing games trying to deter us from his real plan. "There's only one way to find out." He typed in, 'Who is this?' then tapped the send button. "I need to make a few calls. If what's in the message is true, then Shaw is going to let a genie out of a bottle that's a thousand times worse than we could ever imagine."

❋ ❋ ❋

Blake hid at the side of the ranch-style house next to the two-car garage determined to catch Dell Summers are home. There was no chance the man would agree to see him at Flatiron Sargasso, not after Whitney's interview with him or her on-air report. There was a crispness in the early morning air, but things were about to heat up. He rubbed his right temple trying to relieve the signs of a headache. The morning news on the TV wasn't good. Because of Whitney's report, people were already starting to panic, and they were angry, taking to the streets demanding answers from the CDC who continued to remain silent.

He was relieved Sofia was safe in Warm Springs and he and Whitney had spoken to Angel first thing this morning. As sad as Angel was when she'd left the little girl was having a "fun and crazy" time with his parents, McBride, and Cally in Aruba. She'd even asked if she could stay longer. He sure missed the kid, as did Whitney. She was having a hard time dealing with Jerry's death. Speaking with Angel had made a world of difference.

A car door shut.

He edged his head around the corner of the stucco exterior and spotted an attractive woman loading two young children into a car. Moments later the car backed out of the driveway and sped away from the house. He reached for his gun stuffed in the waistband of the back of his jeans and pulled it out. Summers was going to give him the answers he needed.

Blake scanned the neighborhood and high-tailed it to the front door with the weapon tucked close to his thigh out of sight. After knocking, he took a step back.

The door opened half-way and Summers appeared dressed in a white dress shirt and navy pants.

Blake shoved the door open with his palm and pointed the gun at the man's face. "Get inside."

Summers held up his hands and slowly retreated backward then stopped. "Who are you?"

"I'm the guy with the gun." He reached beside him, forced the door shut and locked it.

"If this is a robbery. Take what you want."

"It isn't a robbery. It's an information session. I ask the questions and you answer. Then I won't have to use this." He thrust the weapon at the man's nose.

"Okay. Can I put my hands down?"

"Where I can see them."

The man lowered his hands and kept them nervously at his side.

"First question. Take your time thinking about it because if it isn't the correct answer you and I are going to have a big problem."

Perspiration broke out on Summers' forehead and he nodded.

"Did Matthew Fielding remove a sample of Marburg from the lab?"

The man's eyes darted back and forth rapidly. He was thinking hard about his answer.

"Yes but—"

"Only one?"

"Are you sure?" Blake growled.

"I'm positive. Each specimen is bar coded. Only one was missing."

"How did he become infected?"

"I don't know. He was working in the lab alone. I can

only guess something happened. Maybe a hole in his suit. Nothing was reported to me."

"How did he get the sample out of the lab?"

Summers began to perspire profusely, and Blake jabbed the gun at him again.

"I don't know."

Blake knew he was lying.

"Who was he delivering the sample to at the warehouse?"

"Please. They'll kill my family—my wife—my kids are only four and eight. Please."

His heart sank, and he thought about Angel, and how he would be devastated if anything happened to her. But he needed to know everything the man knew. "I'll kill you if you don't answer."

Summers closed his eyes and shook his head. "Someone named Eduardo."

"Who else is involved?"

"I don't know. It was a different man's voice the last time I got a phone call."

He stared at Summers and continued to read the man's body language. He believed him. "Where's the phone you used to make contact?"

"It's—in my pocket."

"Give it to me."

Summers slid his hand into his pants pocket and pulled out a cell phone.

He grabbed the phone and fired it into his shirt pocket. "What does Nathan Shaw have planned?"

"I really don't know. I was only asked to make sure Dr. Fielding got what he needed out of the facility. If I didn't —they'd kill my wife and kids."

Blake was convinced the man was telling the truth.

Summers was scared to death and he should be. Shaw wouldn't think twice to give the order to kill Summers and his family especially since he'd already gotten what he needed. He reached into his back pocket, pulled a pair of handcuffs and dangled them in front of him. "Put them on."

Summers pushed his shoulders back and held out his chest. "No, I won't. I have no idea who you are. It's bad enough you burst into my house and have a gun on me."

Blake dropped the cuffs and punched Summers in the face. His knuckles cracked hard against the man's chin.

The guy's head snapped sideways.

The asshole deserved the hit and a lot more. He had helped set things in motion by allowing Fielding out of the lab with the sample of Marburg.

Summers wobbled and clutched the side of his face. "You didn't have to do that."

"Yeah, I did. I said put them on."

Summers bent and picked up the handcuffs from the floor. His hands shook as he latched them around his wrists.

Blake lowered the gun and shoved it into the back of his jeans.

"Did Fielding remove any other samples?"

"No. Just Marburg."

Thanks to Summers, Blake knew for sure a sample of another pathogen was probably taken by James Nova from his lab in Texas. He prayed it was only one other agent and not more. It was already bad enough. He hoped whoever emailed Whitney the tip about the chimera virus would contact her again, so they would know exactly what bio-agents they were dealing with.

"What are you going to do to me?"

He wanted to kick the guy's ass for playing a huge part in putting lives in danger, but it wouldn't change anything. It was Nathan Blake wanted. "Help you. It's time to save yourself and your family. I'm taking you to the FBI field office where agents are going to have a chat with you. Tell them the truth. It will go a lot easier for you."

"What about my family? They're going to be in danger if Eduardo finds out I'm talking to the FBI."

Even though Dell Summers was a low-life snake and had played a large role in getting Nathan what he wanted, it didn't mean his family should suffer. "If you tell the FBI everything, and I mean everything, they will help your wife and kids. As for you, you just allowed a madman to create a chimera virus."

CHAPTER ELEVEN

Nervousness cursed through the man's body. He stared at the three-inch-high white aerosol spray bottle with a timer and battery attached enclosed in a small clear plastic case.

The bottle contained death.

He thought about the homeless men and the doctor's assistant, Aleksei. No-teeth was dead, and so was the Smoker. It was difficult to get the gruesome images out of his mind. The third man along with Aleksei was euthanized so they wouldn't suffer.

Dr. Cherenkov's blue eyes flashed. "What we have created here is a true masterpiece. I'm intrigued to see how well the final test goes."

The man was beginning to worry about the doctor's giddiness. Dimitri Cherenkov was an extremely dangerous man. What he could do with biological agents was fascinating and scary as hell. The man looked at the doctor and was glad to be leaving the country soon with his family."

"Will people who have had a smallpox vaccine be affected by the virus?" As far as he knew people in the military were still being vaccinated for smallpox. It would be interesting to see what type of affect Resurrect would have on them.

"They will be. To what extent is not one-hundred-percent clear. The vaccine is only good for ten to twenty years. I don't believe it will really matter if they've been a vaccinated or not. This is a genetically modified virus, a new hybrid microorganism which will evade any known vaccines or treatments. We're in unchartered territory. By the test results of the homeless men, I'd say anyone who comes in contact with someone infected or breathes in the particles will die relativity quickly."

It was exactly what his contact would want to hear. He glanced at his watch. They were ready to go.

Eduardo met them in the hallway carrying a rectangular toolbox. He set the box on the floor and opened it.

"You have two and a half hours." With rubber-gloved hands, Dr. Cherenkov lifted the plastic case containing the virus and placed it in the metal toolbox. He set the timer and closed the lid. "I used a high concentration of bleach to disinfect the outside of the case. But wear gloves just in case. Only a few virons of the virus is necessary. Simply set it in the ventilation system and the detonator will take care of the rest."

At the FBI field office, Whitney sat in Trent Chambers' office feeling exhausted and defeated. Jerry died because of her report. Her stomach rolled with a wave of nausea. She pushed away the pain and guilt and glanced across the desk at Trent. His silver hair looked as if it hadn't been combed for days and dark shadows reflected under his eyes. It didn't appear the man had gotten much sleep after learning about the email she'd received. Neither did she.

"What a God damn nightmare." The man shook his head. "A chimera virus of all things."

Blake leaned against her chair and rested his hand on her shoulder. "Planned and executed by Nathan Shaw. What the hell does he plan on doing with it? There are over one hundred casinos in Las Vegas, three major airports, numerous convention centers, hotels, and events going on in the city."

Chambers shrugged. "I have no clue, but we need to find out. I spoke with on our scientists early this morning. Got the poor guy out of bed. He said if he were going to design a new virus he'd use Marburg along with either anthrax or smallpox due to their highly infectious components."

This was getting scarier by the minute. What had Nathan done, and why? Whitney couldn't imagine another human in the world filled with so much hate as Nathan. The man was the devil.

"We don't have enough to arrest Shaw."

"That's because he has everyone else doing his dirty work. We do have enough to bring him in for questioning and rattle his cage," Blake said. "But it's going to cost the three of us in the room."

Trent's eyebrows raised, and he appeared confused. Whitney knew exactly what Blake was talking about and the thought scared her as much as the chimera virus did.

"I know Shaw better than anyone. He'll threaten again to expose Angel to the media and this time he'll make good on it. I guarantee it. It will be his smack in our faces for bringing him in."

Trent said nothing for a few minutes. "It's a risk we're going to have to take. A whole city could be affected if Shaw uses the virus. I think that cancels out the other for now."

As much as Whitney didn't want to agree with Trent, he was right. A lot of people could die. They'd have to deal with Nathan's repercussions. It was a losing situation either way.

"I pulled Hal and Angela from Warm Springs and replaced them with a couple US marshals. We need as many hands-on deck here as possible. As soon as they arrive, pick up Shaw. I'll notify the Department of Corrections." He snatched the phone and made the call.

While Trent was on the phone, Blake had a grin of satisfaction on his face. He was happy about going to get Nathan. But bringing the man in wasn't going get them any answers. He'd deny everything just as he had in the past.

After he finished the call, Trent hung up the phone and leaned back in his chair. "Mike's in talking to Dell Summers to see if he can get more out of him."

"What about the guy's wife and kids?"

"Agents are rounding them up. We'll put them in protective custody until we figure out what to do with them."

Whitney looked at Trent. "What about the CDC? Ignoring what has happened isn't going to make it go away."

"The director still hasn't returned any of calls."

She let out a sigh. "I still don't understand why they haven't issued a statement. My report should have triggered one. Three infected men with Marburg should have as well. For heaven sakes. People are panicking and protesting outside Flatiron Sargasso Laboratories. It's only going to get worse."

"I know. The local cops are having a hard time keeping order. People want answers. Hell, I want answers. This runaround by the CDC is getting old and will cost more lives." Chambers leaned forward. "I sent two agents to Texas to look for answers as to what agent was taken from Genomics BioMedical. I also spoke with Vic. The Whiz Kid traced the email you received to a 'use and go' service out of Colombia."

Blake pulled out the chair next to Whitney and sat down. "It's the same email service Pablo Sanchez and Cortez Guerrero used to communicate when they kidnapped Whitney. The Whiz Kid told us the service was in stores and coffee shops around the world and was a safe and discreet way to communicate with people who want to hide their identity from prying eyes."

Whitney remembered the Whiz Kid. He was a lanky man who looked as if he should be in the last year of high school not working for the FBI. "Then that rules out Dell Summers as the sender of the email." Frazzled nerves were on edge and concern grew. She didn't know anyone in Colombia. Baffled, she nervously swallowed and turned to Blake. "Could it be from one of your contacts?"

"No. Anyone I know would call me directly. We need to locate Eduardo Diaz. He's our connection to Colombia."

"Immigration said this is his first trip to the US. Diaz stated he was here on a ten-day vacation. I have someone working on finding out if he has family or friends in the country. It might be our best lead."

Blake shoved his hands in his pockets. "This is Vegas, a perfect vacation get-a-way. No one would question it. When did he arrive?"

"Seven days ago, according to immigration."

"Whatever Shaw is planning is going to happen within the next three days. It doesn't give us much time."

The tension in the room thickened. They had three days to stop a madman's plan when they had no idea what the plan was. Time was running out.

The door opened, and Mike walked in followed by Hal and Angela.

"I couldn't get anything new out of Summers," Mike said. "Either he doesn't know anything else or he's one hell of a liar. He seemed genuinely stunned and concerned about the chimera virus. Robson is taking a go at him."

"How's Sofia?" Whitney asked Hal.

"She's fine, adapting okay. She and Fielding's daughter are getting along great. New BFFs." He glanced at Blake and smiled. "She said to tell you and Whitney she missed you both."

Whitney's heart squeezed. She missed her too, and Angel. She couldn't wait until all of this was over to have her family back. The only way it was going to happen is if Nathan was dead. He'd divided them for the last time.

"We drove past the lab on the way in. The protest is growing. There are hundreds of angry people outside the gate demanding answers about the outbreak. Can't really blame them. Traffic is backed up in the area," Angela said.

Chambers stood and leaned against the side of his desk. "Homeland Security, NSA, and the CIA were notified right after I spoke to Blake last night. Until the CDC steps up and makes a statement to confirm what we already know it's going to get worse."

Whitney thought about the chimera virus. She doubted Eduardo had the know-how or expertise to create a virus and neither did Nathan. There were others involved. "Maybe we're looking at this the all wrong. Nathan would need someone to make the virus. A scientist."

"And somewhere to make it." Blake looked Trent. "ShawBioGen. It's the perfect place."

"Christ. He could be producing it right under our noses and possibly selling it to a foreign country," Hal said.

"Go bring the asshole in for questioning." Chamber's eyes shifted to Hal and his voice turned stern. "Play nice. We need him alive. Angela and Mike, I want you to start checking databases for local scientists. Also, see if any foreign scientists have entered the country recently, within the past year."

"Whitney's coming with Hal and me."

Chambers waved his hand at Blake. "Fine. Just stay out of trouble. I think we have enough to deal with. In the meantime, I'll work on getting a search warrant for ShawBioGen. We might have enough for probable cause considering the circumstances and the high risk to the public."

As Whitney followed Blake and Hal to the door, her cell phone dinged signaling an email. Her heart skipped a beat.

Blake stopped dead and Hal bumped into him.

She jammed her hand into her purse, retrieved the phone, and scrolled to the new message. There was a quick intake of breath. A hesitation. What she read forced the breath from her lungs and she swallowed down the panic rising inside her. Whitney glanced up at Blake, and then back to her phone.

Angela touched her arm. "What's wrong?"

Whitney struggled for the words and held up the phone, so Blake could read the screen. "It—it's the answer to the email 'Who is this?'"

His eyebrows raised as he read the reply out loud. "Your father."

* * *

The man wasn't feeling extremely comfortable tagging along with Eduardo, but the job required two people to make it appear as realistic as possible. They didn't need anyone asking questions especially the numerous security guards positioned inside the casino. Besides, if something happened to Eduardo, the man would have to step up to make sure the test was done.

As his friend steered into the Four Spades parking lot, he thought about the virus secured in the toolbox in the back of the van. Dr. Cherenkov had assured him they were safe unless of course something went wrong, and they weren't out of the building in time before the timer went off. Eduardo had already paid one of the staff two thousand dollars to make sure the central air conditioning system wasn't functioning properly. All they needed to do was get in, place the case containing the virus in one of the ventilation ducts and repair the fixable malfunction on the electrical panel.

After parking, the two men walked through the double front doors of the Four Spades dressed in navy blue work shirts with short sleeves and ballcaps. The ceiling lights were subdued allowing the radiance of hundreds of slot machines. The brightly colored machines robotically clanked, dinged, and beeped, the sounds mixing with upbeat music coming from the casino's speakers. It was busy and noisy, and the steamy air was electrified with over three hundred winners and losers.

A security guy glanced at the badges on their blue work shirts then wiped the wetness from his forehead with the back of his hand. "It's about time you guys showed up. It's got to be ninety degrees in here. It's sure not good for business overall but it keeps them lined up at the bar ordering drinks."

The man handed him a white business card with the name Legacy Air Conditioning Repair printed on it. "Sorry about the delay. We had to make a quick pit stop and grab a new part just in case." He spotted the dome cameras partially concealed by a colorful mural of an ancient castle on the ceiling.

"So, you already know what's wrong?"

"Pretty much by the description, we were given," Eduardo said.

"Then I guess it won't take too long."

The man shot him a smile. "We'll have you up and running before you know it." He checked his watch. Eleven-forty-five. They had fifteen minutes before the timer detonated the virus. They were cutting it close. Too close for his liking. "We'd better get to work. We've got two more calls to do before noon. The boss doesn't like it when we're running late."

Security-guy jerked his head toward a door marked 'Employees Only'. "I'll take you over."

Eduardo and the man followed him down three hallways to a large maintenance room. There weren't any cameras in the hallway. He didn't expect there would be, which made their job easier.

Loud chatter on security-guy's radio announced an issue in the casino.

Right on time. The guy wasn't aware the problem had been instigated by some of Eduardo's associates.

"I need to go. We've got a big issue on the floor. A party of six drunks that need to be escorted out."

"We'll be fine. Everything we need is here." He pointed to the electrical panel. "Shouldn't take more than ten minutes. We'll let ourselves out when we're done."

Security-guy nodded and rushed out of the maintenance room.

The man closed the door and surveyed the area for cameras. When he didn't find any, he kept his voice low, almost to a whisper. "We must hurry."

Eduardo set the toolbox on the floor, opened it, and got to work. Once he had a hole cut with tin snips in the sheet metal ductwork he put on a pair of rubber gloves and carefully set the plastic case containing the virus inside.

The man checked his watch.

Seven minutes.

"Hey. What are you doing?"

The man froze and so did Eduardo.

The security man was back, and he didn't appear as friendly this time around at least not by the gruff tone of his voice. He tilted his head to one side and stared at Eduardo's gloved hands with a suspicious look on his face.

"We're just finishing," the man said. He could tell the guy wasn't buying it.

He reached for his radio.

They didn't have time for any complications.

Five and a half minutes.

The man eyed Eduardo signaling him to make a move. They didn't have a choice. They needed to get out of the casino.

As the security guy was about to hit the talk button on his radio, Eduardo reached for the suppressed Beretta 92FS tucked in the back of his pants and fired. The bullet hit the guy in the center of his forehead, knocking him backward. The back of his head smacked against a wooden shelf with a loud crack and he sank to the floor.

The man checked the time again. His heart thudded. "We've only got four minutes."

His friend jammed the gun back in the waistband of this pants and covered it with his work shirt. He proceeded to tear off four strips of duct tape hastily with his teeth and covered the hole in the ductwork to guarantee a large amount of the virus stayed trapped within the ventilation system.

Three minutes.

Four large steps and Eduardo was at the electrical panel quickly repairing the partially cut wire. He flicked on the circuit breaker connected to the air conditioning unit. It hesitated and then hummed.

Once they made it through the hallways unnoticed, they entered the casino floor and slowed their pace not wanting to attract any unwanted attention then briskly walked out the front door.

A wall of cool fresh air hit the man's face and he breathed a sigh of relief. He and Eduardo sprinted through the parking lot and hopped into the van. The man eyed the red digits on the clock on the dashboard.

Sixty seconds.

He rammed the key into the ignition and stomped the gas pedal to the floor.

* * *

Whitney's stomach contracted into a tight ball. She was on edge. Shocked. Confused. Part of her wanted to believe it was true, that her father was alive.

Robert Steel had disappeared while working on a story about the Revolutionary Armed Forces of Colombia and the National Liberation Army. At first, it was believed one of the two left-wing militant groups had kidnapped him. As days dragged on, each one blending into the next, and a ransom demand never arrived, hope faded and turned to fear. She became obsessed, searching for answers, gathering information, not sleeping, not eating, praying she could find him. It never happened. Weeks passed, and the little hope Whitney had left vanished. Then she received news he'd been killed by militants with no further details. She'd buried her father's remains in Florence, Oregon next to her mother.

"Shaw's toying with you. It wouldn't surprise me if he was the one who told Alejandro Quintero to play along with his little game. Both men were involved in your kidnapping and both mentioned your father."

"If it is really Nathan behind the email."

He grasped her hand and held it tight. "It is. Don't let Shaw get inside your head. He's a pro at it. We both know that."

"He's right. The sick asshole would say anything to aggravate you," Hal said, from the back seat.

Whitney had enough of Nathan's twisted games. It was another way he touted his control. If he wasn't plotting to have someone kill the people in her life he was messing with her head, trying to destroy her emotionally, making her question everything in retaliation for her part in putting him behind bars. Her fingernails dug into the palm of her hand and she fought to reign in her anger.

She stared out the tinted window and watched the traffic speed by in the opposite direction. Her mind bounced in every direction. Whitney didn't know what to think. She wanted to retreat somewhere so she could think clearly but she didn't have time. Many lives were at stake if they didn't figure out what Nathan was up to with the virus. But what if her father was alive? Why hadn't he contacted her? So many years had gone by and not one word. There weren't any good options here. Whitney knew that. No matter what she did, she'd lose. The harder Nathan worked at kicking her down the more determined she was to uncover the truth. She needed to find out for herself.

Blake steered the black FBI SUV in the driveway of Nathan's home and parked.

Dread filled her, and nerve endings vibrated. The thought of having that monster in the same vehicle made her want to kill him, for Jerry, and everyone else he'd taken from her. She inhaled a deep breath and let it out slowly and evenly determined to quiet her nerves.

"I doubt he's going to come with us quietly especially without a warrant," Hal said, as he exited the vehicle.

"I'll help him make the right choice," Blake said.

Once they were ushered inside the house by the butler, Nathan greeted them.

"Miss Steel. It's always a pleasure to see you. Did you bring the child with you?"

Bile rose in her throat and turned her mouth bitter. Whitney wanted to drop kick him, make him pay for Jerry's death. She forced herself to remain silent, fighting the urge to pull out the gun from her purse and shoot him. As much as she wanted to, she'd be no good to anyone in prison. Instead, she clutched her hands in front of her.

"We're taking you in with us to the FBI field office. Your friend Dell Summers has had a lot to say about a missing sample of Marburg and your involvement in the production of a chimera virus. We also know you're using one of the labs at ShawBioGen to make the virus," Blake said.

Nathan laughed. The irritating nasal sound trickled throughout the room and drummed in her ears.

"That's absurd. The only contact I've had with Mr. Summers is in regards to my charitable donation to his lab. I believe we've had this conversation before. But I'd be happy to answer any questions. It would be wonderful to leave the house and go for a leisurely drive. A change of scenery is good for the soul. I do need to contact my lawyer first so he can meet us there."

Hal stepped forward, towering in height over Nathan. A vein throbbed visibly in his forehead. "You can call him when we get there."

"No." He glared at his butler. "Call my lawyer. He'll know what to do."

Whitney was disgusted. Very characteristic Nathan behavior. Always defiant. Doing whatever the hell he pleased.

"An innocent man doesn't need a lawyer," Blake said. "But we both know you aren't innocent."

Nathan smirked. "An innocent man always protects his rights. Remember, I agreed to go with you."

"Then let's go." Hal grabbed Nathan's arm and pushed him past her.

Nathan's eyes shifted and flicked. He looked her straight in the eye and said, "I was sorry to hear your cameraman was killed. You can never be too careful these days."

An uncontrollable wave of anger hit, overwhelming, unstoppable. Whitney raised her hand and she slapped him hard across the face. "You had Eduardo Diaz kill

Jerry. You masterminded the explosion at the garage that killed six people and you're the one who sent me an email pretending to be my father. My dead father. You're sick. You'd better watch yourself because you can't be too careful."

"Are you threatening me?" He laughed again. "I have no idea what you're talking about. You're beginning to sound too much like your husband. I always thought you had more smarts and class."

Blake rammed his hands in his pockets. "Get him the hell out of here before I kill him."

Hal yanked Nathan's arm and dragged him out the front door to the vehicle.

* * *

Whitney stood on the other side of the two-way glass and listened to Blake question Nathan. She broke out in a cold sweat. Mike and Angela were on either side of her waiting for Mike and Trent to return with a warrant to search ShawBioGen.

"What other agent are you using for the virus?"

"This is really getting old, Blake. I don't know anything about a virus. Why do you continue to fabricate stories in hopes of putting me back in prison? There is no truth to anything you've said."

She could tell Blake was getting more and more frustrated by the level of his voice and his set jaw. It was going nowhere. The man wasn't going to admit to anything let alone help them.

Blake smashed his fist down on the table. "Why would Dell Summers specifically name you?"

Whitney knew he was trying to trip Nathan up since Dell Summers had never mentioned his name. It wasn't going to work. Nathan was too smart.

"This isn't some make-believe story and you know it, Shaw. People will die. Not that you give a crap about anyone except yourself. Now, who else is involved besides Diaz and some of his men? What do you plan to do with the virus?"

Nathan rolled his eyes. "Mr. Summers wouldn't name me based on one simple fact—it's not true. I know you well, Blake. I know how you operate and I know what makes you tick. Do you want to play good cop, bad cop next? Seems to me you are simply harassing me because I was released on bail. You don't have anything on me but I certainly have something on you, don't I?"

Her stomach sank. And there it was. The veiled threat to expose Angel to media.

"My lawyer will be here soon. I'm not answering any more of your ridiculous questions. Perhaps you get me a cup of the FBI's lovely coffee while I'm waiting." He smiled. "Say hello to our Miss Steel. I know she's behind the two-way glass."

Blake left and met with the others in the adjoining room.

"Shaw is full of shit. He knows exactly what's going on. He planned every detail," Hal said.

"This is the first time I've seen him in action. He's a real piece of work. I'm amazed Blake didn't knock him out of the chair and across the room. I certainly would have," Angela said.

Hal grinned. "I would have too, and then some."

Whitney thoughts turned to Jerry and sadness tugged at her. She was used to having him beside her most of the time, missed having him around. His body was going to be flown to his sister in Washington and buried him next to his father. Whitney wouldn't be able to say goodbye to him.

"A piece of work is an understatement. Nathan Shaw is a psychopath. He'd kill any of us in this room in a heartbeat but not before he made sure we suffered for a very long time. That's exactly what he has been doing to Blake and me for years."

"Whitney's right. The bastard is nuts." Blake kissed her on the cheek and continued to watch Nathan through the glass. "He isn't going tell us a thing. We'll keep him here until his lawyer shows up."

"Who's his lawyer?" Angela asked.

"A big-time scumbag," Hal said. "He got Shaw off death row. He's as much to blame for what's going on."

Blake leaned against the glass and cracked his knuckles. "Hal's right. Warren Demotteo is a scumbag. Las Vegas' go-to defender of organized crime figures like the former Stardust Casino boss, Mickey Scarfano."

"It wouldn't matter if Nathan was in prison or not he'd still be trying to destroy us, all of us. I wish we knew what he has planned."

Trent walked through the door looking disheveled. His tie was undone, hanging loosely around the collar of his shirt and his pants were wrinkled.

He held up a folded piece of paper. "We got the warrant. I assume he isn't saying much?"

Blake shook his head. "I didn't expect he'd reveal anything."

Whitney breathed a sigh a relief. "Maybe we have a chance to stop him after all."

"I've got a call into Homeland Security. I want a team of their guys to go with you to ShawBioGen in case we need to quarantine the area until the CDC are on-scene.

The HERT's team will support you. You're going in blind, not knowing what you're going to find."

Blake glanced at Whitney. "The Hazardous Evidence Response Team collects evidence dealing with the criminal use of radiological, chemical, nuclear and biological materials. In this case, unknown toxins."

Trent eyed Angela. "Did you and Mike find anything?"

"There are forty-six scientists living in the Las Vegas area who would possibly have the expertise to make this type of virus. Thirty-five of them work at Flatiron Sargasso Laboratories. No foreign scientists have entered the US in the past five years. Mike's running background on the local ones."

"Looks like Slick has arrived." Blake gestured his head to the interrogation room at Nathan's lawyer.

Warren Demotteo, a wiry man with an oval face and glossy chestnut colored hair strutted in escorted by two FBI agents. He was dressed in an expensive designer charcoal-gray suit and starched white shirt. Around his neck was a trio of thick gold chains.

Nathan stood and stared directly at her through the two-way mirror. "It's been a pleasure. I won't forget your little slap across the face, Miss Steel." He followed his lawyer and the agents out of the room.

Whitney clenched her jaw tight to stop herself from saying anything. She wouldn't give Nathan the satisfaction.

"I'd like nothing more than to see the cocky asshole back on death row," Blake said.

She couldn't think of a better place for Nathan other than six feet under. "Wouldn't we all."

"With any luck, we'll find what we need at ShawBioGen so we can stop whatever insane plan he has cooked up. Blake. You run point since you're the most familiar with the layout of the facility. It's your show. Make it count." Trent checked his watch. "It's two-fifteen. Meet back here in two hours. To be safe I want everyone wearing disposable field biosafety suits. You could be walking into a trap."

CHAPTER TWELVE

Blake inhaled deeply and sucked in the cool evening air. The sun was about to set, the remnants of what was left of the brilliant orange glow hovering tight along the horizon. As he steered the SUV onto the dirt road two hours northeast of Las Vegas, between Alamo and Mesquite, he spotted the thirty-foot-high security fence surrounding ShawBioGen's million-square-foot concrete and steel compound. The place always reminded him of a state super-prison dumped in the middle of the Nevada desert. He glanced in the rear-view mirror at the entourage of bouncing headlights; dark colored vehicles trailing behind filled with FBI agents, Homeland Security agents, and HERT members.

Whitney sat in the passenger seat, quiet. He was worried about her. They'd stopped at a diner to grab something to eat and she'd barely forced down a few bites. He hadn't thought the past few days could have gotten any worse, but they had with Jerry's death. Adding to the misery the email Whitney had received pretending it was from her father just showed how far Shaw would go. He was a grand master of manipulation. The message was nothing more than a sick and bent charade sent by a demented monster.

Outside the main gates of the complex, Blake threw the vehicle in park.

Whitney pushed a loose strand of hair behind her ear. "This is the last place on earth I thought we'd ever be again."

"I never wanted to come back either. And here we are. At least we got Angel away from this place, away from Shaw. I can't believe he had that sweet child hidden away for three years before we came along. We are going to stop him this time too."

"Thank God she's with us now. Angel sounded happy and excited when I spoke to her and as did Sofia. I miss them. I can't wait until our lives are back to normal."

He grasped her hand and kissed it. "Me too."

"We have to stop Nathan. There are a lot of lives at stake. What do you think he's planning on doing with the virus?"

"Plotting an attack of some sort. Who it's directed at or where is a mystery. We have to stop him before it's too late." The same sinking feeling he had in the pit of his stomach mirrored in Whitney's eyes.

He ignored the retinal scanning device, one of a half-dozen Shaw had ordered him to install when Blake had worked undercover, knowing they weren't going to get into the facility that way and pushed the intercom button. He hung his head out the window and spoke into the speaker. "FBI. We have a warrant to search the premises." Thirty seconds later the gates spread open. He put the SUV into drive and drove in slowly.

The grounds looked the same as he remembered, clogged with cacti, boulders, decorative grasses, and tumbleweed. His eyes adjusted to the eerie shadows surrounding each of the octagon-shaped on-site living quarters as he motored past. Ahead, he spotted the hulking silver metal "S" shadowing the main entrance of Shaw-BioGen. On the rooftop heliport sat the company's helicopter. He steered into the parking lot to the left of the building crowded with hundreds of vehicles and shut off the engine.

He did a quick mic test then tapped his earpiece. "Get suited up. No one goes in unless they're protected."

After twenty-five men and women were geared up in black biohazard suits, gloves, and booties made of Tyvek they put on their full-face respirators complete with HEPA filters. Each team leader carried a large black metal case loaded with hand-held immunoassays (HHAs) and other equipment used to detect biological threat agents including anthrax, plague, smallpox, and Marburg. The units weren't one-hundred-percent accurate, but they were the best they had. Two portable decontamination showers had been assembled outside the front door of the complex just in case they needed them.

Blake clutched the thick handle of one of the cases and he and Whitney walked through the revolving tinted doors. His nerves tightened. Failure to stop Shaw wasn't an option. Too many people would die if the bastard released the chimera virus. His heart beat pounded in double-time. Blake shook off the unsettling thought and came to a halt under the skylight in the main entrance. Water rushed over a waterfall in the middle of the space. Behind the trickling water, highly polished stainless-steel walls created a never-ending mirror. To the right was the area marked, "Security."

The door flew open and a stocky dark-skinned man barreled out dressed in two-tone brown army fatigues. "What the hell is this? What's up with the suits?"

Blake handed him the warrant.

The man read the paper. An eyebrow arched, and a baffled expression crossed his face.

"No one leaves this building. Do you understand?"

The man nodded. "I'll have our security guys secure all the exits."

"Have all employees moved to the cafeteria. What's the access code to the labs?"

Army-guy hesitated. Blake wasn't in the mood for games. He narrowed his eyes at the man.

"Four-two-nine-six-eight."

Blake repeated the code in his mic. "Keypad access is four-two-nine-six-eight. Johnson. Have your team take the lab in the west corridor."

"Roger."

"McCain, your emergency response guys take the west. There are two smaller labs there. Make sure every-thing is swabbed and tested. We need evidence. Every-one check-in with the test results as we go."

McCain's growly low voice rumbled in his ear. "Roger that."

"Mike, Hal, and Angela come with us. We'll hit the south corridor. Shaw's old cloning lab."

Hal's eyes were wide as his head swiveled back and forth. "This place is massive."

"It's going to be a long night," Mike said.

His gut was vibrating telling him they to get this done as quickly as possible. Moisture settled along his hairline and his palms grew damp inside the gloves.

They trekked down the expansive corridor, the suit was hot and sticky against his skin. Blake stopped out-side the cloning lab. "This is it."

Hal punched the code into the keypad. The metal

doors slid open.

After Angela did a quick search to make sure no one was inside, Blake opened the second door at the back of the lab and headed inside. Whitney followed him in.

A rainbow mural was plastered on the wall behind the fancy bed with a toy box at the end. The weird-eyed weirdo had kept everything the way it was when he and Whitney rescued Angel, right down to the pastel painted walls and colorful fabrics.

The sight tugged at his heart.

Whitney glanced at him with a look of disbelief in the back of her eyes. "He never had anything changed."

"This is where he kept Angel hidden all those years?" Angela poked her head inside the door. "Jesus."

Blake fought to keep his voice neutral, anger soaking through his veins. "She was locked away, never allowed outside this lab." His thoughts drifted back to the first time he'd met Angel.

The blonde-haired little girl sat on the edge of an ornate canopy bed with her tiny legs crossed at the ankles. A pink stuffed bunny lay across her lap.

He pushed the memory aside along with his emotions, so he could get this job done.

"The guy is one sick prick." Hal shook his head. "Good thing you guys got the kid out of this place."

Sick was an understatement. Blake set the case on the floor and opened it, revealing a dozen hand-held immunoassays units, containers of swabs, bottles of liquid suspension, and boxes of test strips.

"Let's get to work. Hal, Mike, and Angela already know how to use these, but you don't." He picked up one of the units and gave it to Whitney. "HHAs are small test strips.

They contain antibodies of a specific biological agent. The suspect sample is suspended in the liquid supplied with the test assay. Liquid suspension is then applied to the test strip. It takes about fifteen minutes before we know if a biological agent is contained within the sample. A colored band will appear on the strip if it's positive and tell you which agent it's found. If you get a positive result. Test it again to confirm."

A spark of fear flickered in her eyes and she nodded.

As two hours turned into four, and then eight, exhaustion and frustration grew. They'd searched the entire building as well as all the living quarters. By ten-thirty they had collected over fifteen hundred test samples taken from the five labs in the complex and found nothing.

Blake wrenched off the respirator and pitched it on one of the workstations, knocking over a row of glass beakers. Glass shattered and scattered across the shiny white floor. Sweat poured down the sides of his face and stung his eyes. He dragged a frustrated hand through his hair. "For Christ sakes. Not even a trace of any biological agent." He contacted everyone else. "Shut it down. There's nothing here."

Whitney removed her mask, her hair slick with wetness. "It doesn't make sense. It should be here. There are only two places he could be making the virus that would have the equipment he needs. Here, or Flatiron Sargasso."

"I don't think Summers would risk using his labs. Robson and I talked to him, threatened him numerous times. He cares about his family's well-being before himself. He would have told us." Mike took off his respirator and unzipped the suit to his waist. "I'll take another go at him when we get back, but I think we're barking up the wrong tree. Shaw has to be producing the virus somewhere else."

"Talk to him again. Then go over the list of scientists again too. Run a check on all the ones working at Shaw-BioGen. Shaw has someone working with him. If we can't find where he's making the virus we have to do the next best thing."

Mike nodded.

"Hal. You and Angela work on locating Eduardo Diaz. All roads lead back to him. Our lives depend on finding him."

Terry Johnson's voice crackled in Blake's earpiece. "We just got word there's been some type of biological attack at the Four Spades Casino. Hundreds are dead."

All the energy left his body. Blake looked at Whitney, and then to Hal, Mike, and Angela. "Things just got real."

✳ ✳ ✳

"What is your assistant doing now?" the man asked Dr. Cherenkov.

"Viktor is amplifying the virus using one of the bioreactors. The sound that comes from the unit is exhilarating. It hisses and hums. It can produce a large amount of the virus in a short amount of time replicating the signature fingerprint over and over. Then he'll dry the virus using metal drying trays and seal the particles."

The man didn't understand a quarter of what the doctor was doing but he found the whole process interesting and intriguing. The glass cylinder-shaped bioreactor was about three feet high and had a heavy-looking metal lid with clear tubes winding in and out of it. There were two bioreactors in the lab sitting on one of the stainless-steel workstations. Both were churning away.

"I assume things went smoothly during the final test?"

Smoothly? It wasn't the word the man would describe the adventure at the casino. Nerve-wracking and tense. They'd barely made it out of the Four Spades before the timer went off. He wasn't going to tell the doctor they had to kill one of the security men. It wasn't Cherenkov's business. "Everything went well. It was easier than I expected."

"The outcome of the test I'm sure has hit many of the media outlets by now. I'm sure it will create mass hysteria with people dropping like flies. I noticed that you seem to have an interest in science. You're always asking questions."

The man hadn't checked the TV or radio reports yet, but the doctor was probably correct. The news of what they had done would produce hysteria much like a terrorist attack.

"Perhaps a little bit. I'm finding this experience—fascinating." *And terrifying.* He had already witnessed the true meaning of human trials.

"Did you know Filoviruses like Marburg and Ebola are among the most lethal zoonotic viruses known to affect humans? Mortality rates are up to eighty percent." The doctor pointed to one of the bioreactors. "Resurrect on the other hand has a one hundred percent mortality rate."

"My contact will be more than satisfied."

"Have you thought about how much of the virus your contact would like? I can produce as much as you like. The sky's the limit." He cleared his throat. "Let me give you an example. Using an aerosol attack with ten kilograms of Resurrect on a city of five-hundred-thousand along with a downwind distance of about one kilometer could cause roughly ten thousand causalities.

"He wants something slightly smaller."

"We can adjust the amount to suit his needs. I believe five kilograms will be sufficient. I should get back in there and help Viktor." He patted the man on the arm. "Things are moving right along on schedule."

✳ ✳ ✳

Whitney's jaw dropped open, and she kept her eyes glued to the breaking news report on the TV.

"There has been a possible biological attack inside the Four Spades Casino located behind the Flamingo on south Las Vegas Boulevard. Details are still coming in."

Nathan did this.

Her hands shook, and she gulped down the hard lump in her throat. Thank God Angel was out of the country and Sofia was three hours away at the safe house in Warm Springs. They'd already spoken to Sofia. The young woman was scared, much like everyone else.

The male reporter's voice quivered as he spoke. "Initial reports confirm over three hundred are dead and hundreds more are sick. Authorities have south Las Vegas Boulevard shut down in both directions from Sands Avenue to east Flamingo Road. The area is under quarantine. Officials with the Las Vegas Police Department have asked residents inside and outside of the area to stay in their homes. If you are inside, move to an interior room on a higher floor. Close all windows and exterior doors and shut down air conditioning or heating systems to prevent air circulation. Cover your mouth and nose with a surgical mask, handkerchief or layers of fabric that can filter air and still allow breathing." The reporter paused before continuing, his hand visibly shaking as he clutched the microphone. "If you're in a car, shut off outside air intake vents and roll up the windows. If you suspect you've been exposed to a biological agent, do not go the hospital where you can infect others. Call the emergency number at the bottom of the screen for assistance."

She glanced at Blake sitting on the couch in Trent's office with his elbows resting on his knees, staring at the screen. It was one-thirty in the morning. Faint darkness shadowed under his eyes. He looked as tired and drained as she felt.

His expression turned to stone. "That bastard. A biological attack in the middle of Las Vegas."

"A command center has been set up inside the hot zone. The CDC's Rapid Response Team is on-site along with various officials from Homeland Security as well as local and state emergency workers. Five other casinos in the area are on lockdown."

Trent Chambers burst through the doorway. Lines burrowed deep across his forehead. "I can't believe this."

Her heart beat accelerated, and she forced herself to stay calm. "Are we safe?"

"We're about eight and a half miles north of the hot zone. If the wind doesn't change its direction we're okay." Trent rubbed his forehead. "It's blowing away from us, to the southwest. The HERT members just left. We should know more soon."

Blake stood, the muscles in his arms were twitching. "I'm going to kill that prick."

There was a long line of people wanting to kill Nathan, including herself. Hundreds of people were dead. She still couldn't believe he released a chimera virus.

Trent plopped down in his chair behind his desk looking defeated. "Hal and Angela are working with Mike to see if there's a connection to Shaw and any of the scientists in Las Vegas or the ones working at ShawBioGen."

"Still no word on Diaz?"

Trent looked at Blake and shook his head. "It's as if the guy disappeared into thin air."

"Shaw will make sure Diaz is kept well hidden. He can't risk Diaz getting caught because it would lead back to him. Christ. We thought we'd seen the worst thing that could possibly happen with the terrorist attack at the Diablo Canyon Nuclear Plant." Blake's gaze shifted from Trent and back to the TV screen. "Four hundred dead. Hope to hell we learn what other biological agent he has used with the Marburg."

Trent's phone rang, the sound startling both her and Blake. Trent grabbed the receiver and answered the call.

Whitney stared out the smoky-tinted window that revealed nothing to the outside world. The moon poked through the clouds for a few seconds then disappeared. To the south, the navigational lights of a helicopter hovered over the area of the hot zone. It drew up sharply, banked, and then churned to the west.

Trent pounded down the receiver. Anger flashed his eyes. "The National Guard has been dispatched to protect the perimeter. They have orders to shoot to kill anyone trying to leave the area."

"More people will die trying to flee. It's only natural to run the other way because of fear," Blake said.

"I'm sure there will be many more deaths. Some people in the casino could have left, went to other casinos, went home or to work and infected others. USAMRIID is on-site, and the army is flying in a TAML unit, one of their high-tech theater medical laboratories. It should be there now."

Whitney felt shell-shocked. So many people had already died. She remembered her interview last year with Colonel Tom Wilson. USAMRIID was the United States Army Medical Research Institute of Infectious Diseases, the only DoD laboratory outfitted to study highly dangerous viruses at Biosafety Level 4. USAMRIID worked in partnership with the CDC and the DoD's Global Emerging Infections Surveillance and Response System to provide rapid diagnostic identification and centralized coordination of virus surveillance.

Nathan would do anything to hurt her and Blake and certainly had in the past but releasing a virus in a casino made absolutely no sense. He wasn't attacking them personally even though that was always his goal.

"Why hit the Four Spades? It's one of the smaller casinos on the strip."

"Maybe it was some type of test before he plans on selling the virus to some foreign country."

"Why sell the virus? He certainly doesn't need the money and it's not as if he's going to be alive much longer. Everything he's done in the past has always been aimed at us in one way or another."

"You have a point—Jesus." Blake grabbed the remote and turned up the volume on the TV.

"...the CDC and Homeland Security have officially confirmed it was a biological attack at the Four Spades. CDC Director Don Greeden also confirmed with us minutes ago, the biological agents used in the attack are Marburg and smallpox. He said whoever is responsible for the attack had genetically modified both agents to make what they call a chimera virus. Director Greeden will be talking more about the virus and how you can protect yourself during a press conference in thirty minutes."

Smallpox and Marburg.

Silence, shock, and fear filled the room. Whitney could feel it, taste it. Images of Angel, Sofia, friends, and colleagues ran through her mind. She swallowed hard and searched for words. She didn't have any.

Blake tossed the remote on the couch. "Now we know what we're dealing with. We need to find Diaz *and* the scientist who created the virus."

Trent kept shaking his head in disbelief. "The lab Shaw used to make the virus is somewhere. I thought for sure you were right about ShawBioGen. It made perfect sense."

Blake looked over at her. "Are you okay? You're pale."

"I'm fine." She wasn't. Not at all. "I'm stunned Nathan would do this, killing all those people. Why?"

"Your guess is as good as mine. I agree it's not his usual plan of attack which makes me wonder what else he's up to."

A man, about forty, with broad shoulders dressed in jeans and a navy golf shirt appeared in the doorway.

"We're loaded up. The choppers will be ready in fifteen."

Trent nodded. "Thanks, Chuck." He glanced at Blake. "You don't have to come—."

"We're both going."

Whitney's attention shifted to the TV and she spotted her name rolling across the bottom of the screen in small letters. The camera panned out and moved behind the reporter where officials were gathering in front of numerous microphones.

"While we're waiting for the news conference to

begin...in other news...Nathan Shaw issued a statement, accusing former FBI Agent, Blake Barnett, his wife Whitney Steel, and the Las Vegas FBI field office of a cover up. According to Mr. Shaw, Blake Barnett and his former SAC, Trent Chambers, buried important details from the public regarding the child Whitney Steel and her husband had adopted recently. He further states the child known as Angel was cloned at ShawBioGen using the technology he'd perfected over the past decade. In his statement, he claims the child is the world's first cloned human, an identical copy of Blake Barnett's dead sister, Claire Barnett..."

Whitney's legs turned to jelly, and she dropped to the couch. Trent's phone rang followed by her cell phone, and then Blake's.

* * *

Five miles directly west of the hot zone Blake watched as agents offloaded the second FBI helicopter loaded with protective suits and other equipment. He had just ended a call with his father who was worried sick about him, Sofia and Whitney after learning about the virus attack at the Four Spades.

Whitney's eyes shifted back and forth taking in the growing commotion around them. "How's Angel?"

"She's fine. We know she's safe."

"I still can't believe Nathan had the nerve to expose the truth about Angel. For God sakes, she's an innocent child."

He spotted Chambers talking to the HERT members. "We both knew Shaw would go to the media. It's the price we paid for bringing him in and questioning him. The bastard timed it perfectly to try to deflect some attention away from the virus attack he masterminded. Like Chambers said on the way in, if asked, deny everything. We'll deal with the problem after this disaster."

As they walked through the staging area, large tent-like structures with canvas protection looked like dark green igloos spread out across the parking lot. Colonel Tom Wilson, a tall and fit man in his late fifties with a glossy bald head greeted them.

"Good to see you again, Whitney. Wish it was under better circumstances."

"I wish it was too. This is my husband, Blake."

Wilson shook Blake's hand. "Come on, I'll give you two the tour and fill you in on what we know at this point. The only good thing we have on our side right now is we're upwind and the sun will be up in a few hours. The virus particles will degrade in the sunlight and dry out. They're forecasting rain in the afternoon which should take care of anything lingering in the air and on outside surfaces. The release inside the casino had a much higher concentration and took a much shorter time for the onset of symptoms, making timely treatment and containment next to impossible."

The massive staging area was assembled in the shopping plaza parking lot located on Spring Mountain Road. The area was lit up with portable lights and buzzed with foot traffic; army soldiers, officers and official-looking types from the various organizations involved. Along the perimeter, fifty or more soldiers armed with M16's were standing in front of cement barricades ready to kill anyone breaching the perimeter.

Blake walked past a row of satellite dishes used for high-speed communication and to access the Internet. He shoved his hands in his pockets. "How many casualties so far?"

"At last count, about thirty minutes ago, six hundred and ninety-six."

Whitney looked at Blake, and then back to Colonel Wilson. "This is unbelievable. Those poor people and their families."

"Unfortunately, more will die. Casualty target estimates are fifteen to eighteen hundred. That's a conservative number considering the type of virus and the unusually quick onset of symptoms." The colonel stopped outside a long tube-like canvas covered building isolated at the far end of the staging area away from the igloo-shaped structures. "This is the level 4 bio-containment field hospital. It has eight emergency beds, two surgical, ten intensive care, and forty-eight ward beds. They're all full. The sick are being transported in through the back where mass casualty triage is set up to assess and categorize each patient. There are decontamination chambers at both ends of the unit. At this point, it doesn't matter how many beds we have. The ones they're bringing in aren't living for more than an hour after they arrive. Most have died before they made it here. I'll warn you. It's not pretty."

Two stone-faced soldiers stood on each side of the entrance of the field hospital door. Blake and Whitney followed Colonel Wilson inside.

After changing into a Level A PPE full body positive-pressure suits with over-gloves and over-boots integrated into the suit, they put on their full-face masks.

The colonel peered at Whitney through the clear visor. "What you're going to see will shake you to the core. You've been warned."

She honestly wasn't sure what to expect. "I'll be

okay."

As they walked through a long tube with its own self-contained ventilation system, the extra weight of the suits slowed their steps. Walls of metal IV poles, x-ray machines, portable ultrasounds and ECG/EKGs lined the white rubber interior of the hallway. Rooms were partitioned off to the left and right with zippered flaps at each entrance. At the end of the hall, they entered the largest room filled with ward beds. Two dozen nurses and doctors in their biosafety suits went bed to bed attending to the sick and dying.

Blake's attention snapped to a young child, about five years old, her shoulder-length brown hair drenched with sweat. Six clear bags of medication in various sizes hung from two IV poles next to the bed. Blood streamed from her nose and the corners of her eyes. Puss filled blisters seeping with greenish opaque liquid deformed her small face and bare arms. Tears formed in the corners of his eyes. Monitors beeped and dinged as convulsions wracked her tiny body. A doctor and nurse worked feverishly to help her, knowing they couldn't save her life.

"All the medication in the world isn't going to help these people. All staff can do is make patients as comfortable as possible. Then when it's time, get their bodies out so they can prepare for the next batch. The bodies are being transported to the basement of empty office building five miles north of here where they are being decontaminated and cremated once their next-of-kin have been notified."

Blake thought he'd seen it all when he was in the Marines. Nothing prepared him for what he'd just witnessed. Nathan Shaw was responsible for everything. He'd sentenced thousands of people to death—killed them all—killed the little girl. *It could have been Angel.* His hands balled into fists. "Have there been *any* survivors?"

"None. It's not likely there will be any either."

Blake had seen enough.

After their suits were doused and scrubbed down twice with spray bleach in the decontamination chamber, the three removed the protective gear and walked out of the hospital.

Whitney stepped outside the door, her face white and sweaty. She stopped, suddenly bent and threw up.

Wilson ordered one of the soldier's guarding back door to get her some water.

Blake handed her the bottle and rubbed her back. "You okay?"

"I think so." She straightened and inhaled and exhaled deep breaths a few times then took a sip of water. "I don't know what I expected to see inside but I wasn't expecting it to be so bad."

Horrifying was the only word Blake could come up with. A few minutes passed, and the color finally returned to her face.

Behind the plaza, an army CH-47 Chinook helicopter hovered high above the roof and lowered another military shipping container to the ground packed with supplies and equipment. Dust swirled in the air. The distinctive *whup-whup-whup* sound of the rotor blades sliced through the night air.

Colonel Wilson pointed to the dome-shaped building across from where they were standing. "The epidemic task force is in there. A team of epidemiologists are monitoring any new cases and will follow up with anyone who had contact with someone infected or any surfaces at the casino. Trent said you think you know who's responsible, but you don't have any evidence to arrest the man."

Blake nodded. "Nathan Shaw. He's working with a Colombian man, Eduardo Diaz, and probably a few others. We're trying to discover the name of the scientist who engineered the virus and find him before something else happens."

"I have someone you'll want to speak with. He might be able to provide you with some specifics about the chimera virus."

"Any information will be helpful. We need to nail Nathan Shaw."

Minutes later, they met up with Chambers inside the biocontainment hub. The back area of the hub was divided from the main space with a thick sealed glass partition and was considered 'hot'. The HERT members were dressed in biosafety suits and were busy working alongside various other organizations collecting and analyzing evidence.

Chambers looked at Blake. "How bad is it?"

"Horrible." He had a hard time getting the words out. "We just watched a little girl die."

"Christ."

Colonel Wilson introduced a short man about fifty years old with thick brown hair and a well-trimmed mustache and goatee.

"This is Dr. John Pierson. He's the chief microbiologist with USAMRIID."

"What can you tell us about the virus?" Whitney asked.

"In ancient Greek mythology, a chimera was a monster made of parts of two different animals. In this case, the virus is made up of Marburg and smallpox. The particles have been coated with a thin layer of plastic so they don't dissipate as quickly in the air."

"That's not much of a bonanza under the circumstances," Chambers said.

"It's not." Dr. Pierson paused briefly. "Both agents were genetically modified using a technique we've never seen in this country before. In 1988, the Soviets froze Dr. Nikolai Ustinov's blood and tissue after he infected himself with Ebola. They replicated the strain and named it Variant U. They mass-produced the virus, dried it, and processed it into an inhalable pink powder that resembled talcum powder. At the time, Variant U was on the brink of being a biological weapon ready to load into MIRV warheads."

Blake raised his eyebrows. "The guy we're looking for is a Russian scientist?

"Yes, I believe so. In the early 90s, Russian scientists found a way to splice Venezuelan equine encephalitis and used DNA from smallpox to create a new chimera virus called, Veepox. Under a microscope, the microorganism looked identical to smallpox. Using Marburg and smallpox is—I hate to say it, brilliant from the standpoint of engineering a biological weapon. Smallpox is highly contagious and is spread through respiratory droplets when a person coughs or sneezes. Marburg on the other hand, requires direct contact, bodily fluids or feces. This new virus is a hot and lethal strain resistant to any antibiotics or viral medications. The smallpox vaccine still may provide some protection even after one to four days of exposure, but the Marburg component of the virus will probably kill them. There's only a small handful of microbiologists in the world who have the expertise to produce something like this."

Blake stepped out of the conversation, retrieved his cell phone from his back pocket and called Mike.

"Yeah."

"Check the databases for Russian scientists who came to the US either recently on a tourist visa or within the last thirty to thirty-five years and never left."

"What exactly am I looking for?"

"Anyone who might have a connection to the Soviet biological weapons program."

CHAPTER THIRTEEN

At six-fifteen in the morning, the man poured a cup of coffee and sat at the table. He'd called his family last night to confirm their bags were packed. His wife was extremely worried to the point of paranoia about the virus attack. Thankfully the wind continued to blow in the opposite direction away from their Las Vegas home.

He looked at Dr. Cherenkov. "They were here last night with a warrant to search the premises."

"Not to worry. No one will find us down here. They're going to check all the labs in the state after the virus release. It's the natural progression of things after something so serious."

The doctor was right. It only made sense the authorities would be searching all labs. "Many of the news outlets are reporting the same casualty numbers this morning. Seventeen hundred and thirty-five dead so far."

"I would say the test was more than successful." The doctor smiled and took a sip of his coffee.

Dr. Cherenkov had a twinkle in his eyes. He was proud of what he'd accomplished; creating the virus and the test results. His contact would be happy as well with the outcome.

"The five glass containers with the virus particles are

almost ready. Some of the particles will be lost due to the small explosions and will weaken in the light. I'll be adding a little extra to make up for what might be lost. I'm waiting for Eduardo to return with the other items you require then we'll get everything loaded in the van. He said he'd send a clean-up team to dispose of the bodies later tonight."

Five kilograms of instant death.

He had already witnessed what a small amount of the virus could do. The thought drove a shiver down the man's spine.

* * *

After downing a poached egg, toast, and a cup of tea, Whitney threw on a pair of blue jeans and a navy tank top while Blake was on the phone talking to Mike.

They'd only had a few hours of sleep; restless, tortuous sleep satiated with nightmares after what'd they witnessed at the staging area. She found some comfort in knowing Blake's parents, Sofia and Angel were safe, but she had no idea if her friends and colleagues were safe. It was the first time since she'd started working at News3 that Travis didn't want her reporting live. He didn't want to put her or any other employees in harm's way. This story wasn't worth it. Enough people had died.

Whitney sat on the edge of the bed and laced up her running shoes. Why had Nathan released the virus in the casino? The attack wasn't aimed at her and Blake like all the other horrible things he'd done in the past. He knew a casino would be the last place her and Blake would be. Why attack innocent people? She wasn't convinced he'd used the virus as some sort of test before selling it a foreign country. It wasn't the way he did things. Not even close. Every move he made was calculated, directed at them. She was dumbfounded trying to figure out the answer.

Blake appeared in the doorway wearing a black T-shirt and jeans. His hair was still damp from their shower together. His usual bright eyes were dull, the lack of sleep taking a toll.

"Mike found only one scientist linked to the Soviet's biological weapon program. Dr. Dimitri Cherenkov. He's our guy. His father was second in command of the weapons program during the '80s. Cherenkov has been residing in the US since 2013. Chambers has already sent a team to search the man's house in Summerlin, about fifteen minutes from the FBI office. I also spoke with Colonel Wilson. The wind is still blowing away from us. Dr. Pierson said the virus particles have dissipated a lot due to the sunlight and warm temperature. New cases seem to be declining slowly.

"At least that's a bit of good news. Maybe the worst is over."

He sat down beside her and kissed her temple. "It's not all good news especially for the people already infected and are unknowingly infecting others. They're predicting the death count could climb to five thousand within the next few days. Chambers said five FBI agents in the area of the hot zone have been infected as well as their families. Not to mention the dozens of first responders. They aren't expected to make it."

The sadness in his voice was undeniable. She leaned her head on his shoulder. "I'm so sorry. I can't believe Nathan did this." She was afraid to turn the TV on again. By nine-thirty the death toll had risen to twenty-five hundred. If what Blake said was right, the number would double. "Why would he risk infecting himself? His house is south of the hot zone."

"He wouldn't. Don't kid yourself. Shaw isn't stupid. He always plans right down to the last detail especially when it involves him. He'd have everything in place to ensure his own safety first and foremost. He probably has a secure room in the house he rented with all the equipment he needs including protective gear. Believe me, the bastard was the only one prepared."

His cell phone rang. The shrill tone grated on her nerves. Every media outlet in the country had been calling continuously wanting to know more about Angel and if Nathan's statement was true that she was the world's first cloned human. Eventually, they would be forced to deal with the issue. He doubted anyone would ever believe a man who had been sentenced to death row. For now, it was the least of their worries.

He plucked the phone out of his shirt pocket. "It's Chambers. I need to take this." He got up and walked out of the bedroom.

Whitney went and stood in front of the mirror and pulled her hair back into a loose ponytail then fastened it with an elastic band. She eyed her cell phone on the dresser. She picked up the phone and scrolled through the emails until she found the one she wanted. She stared at the screen.

Two biological agents. Chimera virus. It's a
genie no one wants let out of a bottle.

If Nathan was the sender, why would he feed her information that could help them? He won't. It would be completely out of character. If anything, he'd make sure she was walking into as much danger as possible. She didn't know who was playing games. It wasn't Nathan and it wasn't her father. Her pulse raced. Whitney tapped the keyboard, the tips of her fingers trembling.

Help me find the lab where the virus was made

Seconds later a message popped on the screen.

ShawBioGen

They'd already searched the facility and didn't find anything.

It's not there

The phone dinged again.

You just have to look hard enough

Whitney gasped, and her mind reeled. Those were her father's exact words.

Her father was dead. It can't be. She'd buried him.

Her vision blurred, and the room spun. She grabbed the corner of the dresser to steady her balance and snapped her eyes shut. Someone was playing a cruel joke. There was no other explanation.

"Chambers said the team didn't turn up anything at Cherenkov's house. Nothing linking him to the virus. The neighbors claim they haven't seen the guy for a couple of days. Chambers issued a BOLO."

Her eyes popped open at Blake's voice.

"Whitney?"

"We need to go back to ShawBioGen."

The urgency in her voice made him pause. "What are you talking about? There's nothing there. None of the samples came back positive. Not a trace of any biological agent."

Whitney glanced over her shoulder at him. "Whoever has been sending me emails hasn't steered us wrong yet." She passed him the phone. "We have to go back. The lab is hidden. We need to search again."

＊ ＊ ＊

Blake refused to believe for one second the lab Cherenkov had used to create the virus was somewhere in ShawBioGen. They'd searched the facility completely the first time. It didn't hurt to be diligent, but he was concerned Whitney was beginning to believe the email messages were from her father. Shaw was taunting her, playing with her head. He paid one of his old friends in Colombia to do it. His jaw tightened. Her father was dead. Dead men don't talk.

"Have all employees been moved out of the facility?"

"Except for the three of us in security."

"Are you certain?"

Army-guy nodded. "Everyone is accounted for in the parking lot. We double-checked."

"They stay put until I say so. Got it? No one leaves."

The man nodded again. "Shouldn't we all have suits on just in case?"

Blake pointed the handheld thermal infrared camera toward the security door. Two dark pink distorted heat signatures popped on the screen. At least the guy was telling the truth. "No. Take your men and get to the parking lot."

"I'm going to have to call Mr. Shaw and let him know what's going on."

Hal glared at army-guy, his large frame hulking over the man. "Naw. Shaw doesn't need to know anything."

"Give me your master keycard." Blake held out his

hand

"What?" The guy's eyes shifted back and forth from Hal to Blake.

"Keycard."

"You can't just come in here and do whatever you want."

"We sure as hell can. The warrant is good for five days. Your boss is the person responsible for the biological attack. You want to end up like the twenty-five hundred already dead?"

Army-guy's eyes widened with surprise. "I didn't know." He hastily reached into his pocket and pulled out the keycard.

Blake handed the card to Hal. "There's a washroom on the south side of the security room. Take him and his two friends and lock them in there until we're done. Make sure the others don't have cell phones or cards on them. We don't need Shaw knowing what we're doing."

Ten minutes later, Hal returned. "Done. They didn't look too pleased."

"They'll survive. It's for their own good and one less thing for us to worry about. This time we start in the basement. We'll break off in pairs, search each floor and work our way back here."

"Nathan would make things as difficult as possible for us. It's concealed. It makes sense why we didn't find it the first time. It's here. I'm positive."

"Hope you're right," Hal said.

Blake hoped Whitney was right too and she wasn't reading too much into the email.

Angela glanced at the black protective suits and respirators in a large cardboard box on the floor. "We'd better suit up."

"And be careful. If the lab really is here there's no telling what Shaw has in store for us."

Once everyone had their headsets and their suits on, Blake and Hal each grabbed a metal case containing the hand-held immunoassays. They trudged through the north corridor to the end of the hall and took the elevator to the basement.

The basement was huge open space. Along the one wall sat stacks of boxes to the ceiling filled with equipment and supplies. Using the thermal infrared cameras to pick up any heat sources Hal and Angela scanned each of the walls and the floor while Blake and Whitney checked the maintenance room from floor to ceiling. Thirty minutes passed and sweat pooled inside his suit. The wetness made his skin itchy and uncomfortable. The sooner he got out of the damn thing the better.

Whitney glanced around at the large space. "There's nothing down here except for a lot of supplies."

He wasn't expecting to find anything. He had a feeling the email was a crock of crap, meant to send them on a wild goose chase. "Hal, you and Angela go back up to the main floor and check the other labs. Whitney and I'll head to the second floor."

"If we find anything we'll let you know."

While Hal and Angela entered the main elevator, Blake and Whitney took the private one marked C2 to the second floor where Shaw's living quarters and office were located. Cameras linked to the security room recorded their move. Blake always thought it was weird the guy had made the facility his home before being tossed in jail considering the billions of dollars he was worth. At the time, it made sense. Shaw wanted to be as close as possible to his illegal human cloning project so he could kill anyone who got in his way.

The elevator dinged open and Whitney stepped into the hallway first.

The overhead florescent lights, shiny white floors, and highly-polished stainless-steel walls were a blinding trio and made Blake's head pound.

Whitney tapped the access code into the keypad. "I don't like being here."

"It's not my favorite place to be either."

The metal doors slid open and shut behind them like a tomb.

Nothing had changed. Plush beige carpet and soft pot lighting lit the office, much different than the stark lighting in the hallway. Two brown and white cowhide covered chairs sat in front of Shaw's large cherry gold-trimmed desk. In the corner of the room was a second wooden desk, smaller, more ornate. A chocolate brown leather sofa was on the other side of the room with a Chippendale coffee table in front of it.

Whitney walked around the room glancing up and down, running the camera along the wall. "Is this the only spot in the complex without cameras? I didn't notice it until now."

"Here and the washrooms. The bastard has always been paranoid about his own privacy. He doesn't care if he invades anyone else's." He walked behind the large desk and pressed the red button on the wall. Across the room, the fully stocked bar swung open revealing dozens of bottles of wine, whiskey, and scotch.

"I've never seen that before."

"Shaw has always liked his booze. Especially expensive scotch. Stuff I can't even pronounce the name of." He spoke into his mic. "Find anything?"

Hal's voice blasted in his ear. "Nothing. I have a feeling we're not going to."

"You might be right. Keep us updated." This was going nowhere quickly.

"I don't see anything that would lead to a lab." Whitney walked behind him and stared at the wood paneled wall.

Blake heard the disappointment in her voice. He wasn't surprised they hadn't uncovered anything.

"Wait."

Blake turned, the suit clinging to his legs.

Whitney moved her gloved hand across a section of the wood paneling. "Something isn't right. This area looks different compared to the rest of the panels." She pointed the thermal camera at the wall. "Nothing."

"Maybe it's just the lighting in here casting shadows. It's not very bright."

"No. I don't think so." She pointed. "It's uneven here at the bottom corner."

He ran his hand against the twelve-by-twelve inlaid square and applied a bit of pressure. He tried the one next to it and then another. The third square clicked and opened, revealing a metal card swipe mechanism. It looked brand new. "Someone is trying to hide something."

"I bet it leads to the lab."

She was probably right. Excitement bellowed in her voice as if she was trying to validate the message in the email. Blake had to admit he was stunned by the find and apprehensive about what they might discover once they accessed the unit.

"Hal. Can you hear me?"

"Yeah."

"We found something in Shaw's office. You and Angela get up to the second floor. Bring Army-guy, a keycard, and the weapons."

"On our way."

Whitney glanced at him. "It looks like it was recently installed."

"The bastard was smart enough to hide it. I'm guessing he had Eduardo install it."

Moments later, Blake turned to see Army-guy, followed by Hal and Angela. Hal was carrying the knapsack with their weapons. He set the sack on the edge of the desk.

"Check this out." Blake pointed to the card swipe system.

Hal stared back at him with wide eyes. "The asshole has been busy even when he's not here."

Blake shifted his attention to Army-guy. "Has there been any construction done recently in the complex?"

"No construction. The only thing that's happened was one of the elevators broke down and needed to be fixed. It took over three months. The repair was finished last week."

That explained when the card swipe was installed, and Blake doubted there was anything wrong with the elevator. A broken elevator was just a way to hide what was really going on.

Army-guy suddenly looked a little nervous. "I really think I should have a protective suit on too."

"Blake flipped open the flap on the knapsack and pulled out a pair of handcuffs. He threw them to Angela. "Secure him so he doesn't get in the way."

Army-guy frowned. "Are you serious?"

The guy was frightened but Blake sensed Army-guy

wasn't telling them the whole story.

Angela snatched the man's muscular arms, jerked them behind him, and cuffed him. "We're serious." She gave him a slight push. "Go sit on the couch and don't move."

Blake pulled out a .40 caliber Smith and Wesson semi-automatic from the knapsack and passed the weapon to Hal. He grabbed the Glock 22 for himself and handed the Sig Sauer P226 to Angela. He passed the Ruger LC9 to Whitney.

Hal handed him the master keycard. "Let's do this."

Anticipation filled the room.

Blake swiped the card and waited. The unit beeped three times followed by a long pause and a flashing red light. He let out the breath he was holding. "It's not going to work." Again, he wasn't surprised. He tossed the card on the floor."

"Nathan wouldn't have the unit programed with the same access code as the rest of the complex. He wouldn't make things easy for us," Whitney said, as she sat on the corner of the desk.

"I'll get some tools, see if we can bypass it. Keep an eye on him."

Hal nodded. "He's not going anywhere."

"He knows more than what he's been telling us."

After Blake returned with a pouch of tools he un-screwed the cover of the unit and inspected the wires. After cutting, moving and reconnecting a few wires he bent down and picked up the keycard. He swiped the card again. The unit beeped, and a green light flicked. Seconds later a portion of the paneled wall slid open exposing a small elevator.

Hal and Angela stepped back a few steps.

He glanced over his shoulder at Army-guy whose expression was unremarkable.

Whitney's eyes brightened. "We're in."

Blake peered inside the elevator and noticed there was only one button to push; down. His stomach lurched. He had a bad feeling in his gut about what they were about to find.

❊ ❊ ❊

Whitney clutched the handle of the Ruger LC9 and a case containing the hand-held immunoassays. There was no way the security man they'd left handcuffed in Nathan's office didn't know what was going on in the complex. He might not have known the exact details, but he knew.

Part of her was still in shock by the email. As much as she wanted to believe it was sent by her father she knew deep down it wasn't possible. Nothing would change that.

Blake pressed the down button. "Be alert. We don't know what we're walking into or who might be down there."

They scrunched into the elevator.

Seconds later, the elevator jolted to an abrupt stop. The doors opened into a well-lit area.

Blake poked his head out first. He looked left, and then right. "It's clear. Whitney and I will take the right." He glanced at Hal and Angela. "Be careful."

Angela held the handle of another case of the immunoassays testers. They both nodded and had their guns ready.

After everyone got out, Whitney stayed a few steps behind Blake, close to the wall, her gun pointed in front of her. The hallway was about seventy-five feet long with unfinished wood framed walls and white linoleum flooring. It looked as if whoever had built it didn't have time to finish the job.

"Army-guy lied to us," Blake said.

"Obviously. It would take more than three months to build this."

"A lot longer. It's not very old. A few weeks by looks of it. This side of the complex backs into the employee parking lot. There must be an exit other than the elevator up to Nathan's office. They had to be able to get in large construction supplies."

She heard Angela's soft voice in her ear. "We found a small kitchen. The coffee is still hot in the pot."

"Keep your eyes peeled." Blake slowed his pace. "There's something ahead of us."

Whitney's heart sped up and she gripped the gun tighter. She noticed the bright light spilling across the floor in front of him.

He turned right and stopped. "Jesus."

When she caught up with him her jaw dropped open at the sight of a large glass window spattered with blood and two perfectly formed bloody hand prints. She lowered her gun. This is where they had tested the chimera virus.

Inside the room, two men lay on the floor and another one was on his back, spread-eagle on a bed. A fourth man was in a biosafety suit curled in a ball on the floor. She had no idea who the man was in the protective suit. Streaked and splattered blood was everywhere; clothing, walls, bedding. Puddles of vomit and other bodily fluids scarred the floor. Fear reached deep in her stomach and rose in her throat. The scene revealed a torturous painful end for the men.

Transfixed by the horror, Whitney couldn't believe what she was looking at. She gulped hard and spotted the men's ratty and worn clothing. Sadness flowed through her. "They look like they were homeless men."

"Eduardo probably plucked them right off the street promising the men something they wanted. I doubt this is anything close to what they expected to get. That guy's biosafety suit is cut open at his legs. Explains why he's dead." He tilted his head to one side. "His face isn't familiar but it's hard to tell with so much blood."

"There's nothing else at our end other than the kitchen and a small washroom. We're heading back to you," Hal said.

"Okay." Blake looked at her. "We'll keep moving."

At the end of the hall, he peered around the corner. "Clear."

Whitney walked beside him, trying to rid the graphic images of the men from her mind, her hands slippery with sweat inside the gloves making it difficult to keep a firm grip on her weapon let alone the handle of the case. It was hard to fathom Nathan was responsible for this as well.

Suddenly a slightly overweight man with a round face appeared out of an open doorway holding a coffee mug in his hand.

Blake stopped.

Whitney aimed the Ruger at the man's chest.

"Don't move." Blake kept his gun pointed at him.

The man looked at them and didn't move.

"We're coming up behind you so don't be shooting us," Hal said.

"Roger." Blake walked to the man. "Put the cup down."

The man bent slowly and placed the mug on the floor then straightened and raised his hands in the air.

Blake trained the gun at the man's head then grabbed his shirt collar and dragged him away from the doorway. "You must be Dimitri Cherenkov. It really sucks to get busted, doesn't it?" He let go of the man's clothing and shoved his back against the wall.

The man's eyes shifted from Blake to her. "Dr. Cherenkov to both of you."

"Where's Eduardo Diaz?"

"I don't know who you're talking about."

Blake held the Glock 22 to man's temple. "I see you've been to the Nathan Shaw school of denial. Sorry, you aren't getting a hallway pass especially after what you did to those men back there and the thousands of others you've killed." He spoke into his mic. "Hal and Angela get that room checked."

Whitney heard the wrath in Blake's voice.

"Got it," Angela said, as she and Hal walked past them with their weapons raised.

"I didn't kill anyone."

"You produced the virus. You're responsible for killing those people as much as Eduardo and Nathan Shaw." Blake kneed him hard in the groin.

The man groaned, doubled over and sank to his knees, holding himself.

After Hal and Angela entered the room, Whitney instinctively glanced over her shoulder, down the hallway, which wasn't easy wearing the respirator mask.

"I think we found the lab," Hal said.

The sender of the email was right. The lab was here, hidden from the world very much like Nathan's human cloning project years before. She didn't understand why he would do something so horrific and deadly, targeting innocent people. But then again, Whitney couldn't figure who was behind the emails either. It certainly wasn't Nathan.

Blake snatched a handful of the doctor's hair and pulled him to his feet. "You and your little friends are going to be spending the rest of your life in prison or maybe with some luck, you'll get the death sentence. This might be a really good time to start talking."

"Like I said. I don't know anyone by the name of Eduardo or this Shaw person. I was only hired to make the virus. Nothing more. What's done with it after it's produced isn't my business or concern."

"There are four bodies back there because of the virus you designed. Who hired you? Why was it released in the casino? Was it a test before Nathan Shaw sells the virus to a foreign government?"

"My only job was to make it. I was never given the name of the person who hired me."

Whitney had a feeling he was partially telling the truth. "Nathan would never give out his name for fear it would lead back to him."

"Well look what I found. A slimeball."

She couldn't believe her eyes. Nathan's lawyer? Blake had the same look of shock on his face as she probably did.

Hal had Warren Demotteo's arm twisted behind his back. He wrenched the man's arm up higher and Whitney heard a defined crack, like a branch snapping in two. "Donahue's in the lab testing samples. There are change rooms and decontamination showers back there too."

Demotteo eyes bulged and he howled in pain. "You broke my arm."

"A broken arm is better than what I'd do to you." Blake pressed the barrel of his gun into the man's forehead. "Shaw has you, Cherenkov and Diaz doing his dirty work. Now it makes sense. Where's Diaz?"

It did make sense. Everything except for why. She still couldn't grapple with why Nathan had killed so many people.

Demotteo shook his head. "I have nothing to say." His eyes flicked to the end of the hallway then to Blake.

Whitney spun around.

Eduardo's eyes met hers.

He turned and took off running in the opposite direction.

She dropped the metal case and ran. *Don't let him get to the elevator.*

"Whitney, wait!" Blake yelled.

Her feet hammered, the rubber of the over-boots squeaking against the linoleum floor. She was keyed-up, adrenaline blasting through her veins. Whitney slowed when she got to the corner of the hall and jammed her back against the wall, two-handing her gun. Sweat rolled down her forehead and dripped down her face. She inhaled and exhaled then cautiously stepped around the corner.

Eduardo punched her wrists hard.

The gun flew out of her hands and hit the floor, spinning like a top, out of reach.

He stared at her with intense wild dark eyes and never said a word.

She had to gain control before he hit the elevator button. If she didn't, he'd be long gone.

Whitney moved like lightning, fast and fluid, landing a double palm heel blow to both his ears imagining her hands penetrating his brain. While his hands flew to his head, her elbow connected under his chin, his body jerking to the same rhythm of each of her blows. She positioned her feet and legs to do a reverse roundhouse kick when Eduardo twisted sideways, and she lost her balance. He reached into his pocket and pulled out a switchblade and thumbed the release. The knife sprung open and he side-eyed the elevator button.

Her eyes followed his and he caught her off guard. He was quick. Far too quick.

The blade slashed through her suit and cut her arm. When she glanced at the blood oozing from the wound, he kicked her in the stomach and knocked her backward onto her back. The air sucked from of her lungs and she saw stars in the back of her eyes. Whitney gasped small breaths trying to catch her breath and heard the elevator door open, and then close.

* * *

Stars illuminated in the clear night sky as if brilliant diamonds had been hurled to the heavens like glitter. It was different out here in the desert, dark, vast, open. A light wind whispered across Blake's face, the coolness of the air refreshing after being stuck in the biosafety suit. He was exhausted mentally and physically. He ran a hand over his face.

They'd taken two long chemical showers to decontaminate their suits. The smell of the tangy bleaching agent was embedded in his nostrils. They'd discovered another elevator that led to a door opening out to the back employee backing lot. They would never have known the door existed by the way the facade of the complex blended in perfectly. The lab had been located two floors below Shaw's office. Blake stared at the towering 'S' outside of ShawBioGen. Hard to believe the bastard had gone to so much trouble to destroy so many lives. For what?

"Are you sure you're okay?"

Whitney leaned against him. "I'll be fine. The EMT patched up my arm. It doesn't need stitches. It's sore but I'm okay. At least I got a good couple of hits in before Eduardo took off."

Blake was glad she was okay. He didn't know what he'd do if anything had happened to her. "Well, you don't have to worry about being infected. The HERT members tested all the samples they gathered twice. The only area that was hot was inside the lab where Cherenkov and his assistants produced the virus. The construction of the lab was top of the line, ten times safer than our government and military BSL-4 labs. Shaw had to have spent millions." He was relieved and could see the relief on her face as her features softened.

"He had assistants?"

"Yeah. Viktor Morozov. We think he got away with Diaz. We'll find them both. A BOLO was sent out. There's no way they're getting out of the country. The man in the biosafety suit was Cherenkov's second assistant. We don't have to worry about him. His name was Aleksei Petrov, a Russian microbiologist, and chemist whose family had been living in the US for the past twenty years."

"All these men have been living here for decades. That's a scary thought."

"It is. Hal said Diaz put a bullet in Army-guy's head when he fled the complex. I guess he was concerned the guy would talk. He sure-as-hell knew a lot more than he was willing to tell us. The local cops spoke with some of the employees and confirmed the construction at the complex started last summer. The ones they spoke with were shocked to learn what was going on inside."

"It's certainly not something you hear about every day."

"Chamber's is still questioning Cherenkov. He doesn't think he'll get much more out of him. He's tight-lipped. Hopefully, he'll break him. Hal and Angela are on round two with Demotteo and forensics are going over his financials. I'm positive there's a huge payoff somewhere." His throat tightened. "They have to find the connection to Shaw. Demotteo's family was brought in and were questioned. When agents searched their house, suitcases were already packed waiting at the front door. They were prepared to disappear."

"I can't believe Nathan's lawyer is in on this too. Why would his lawyer do something like this? All the people that have died..."

Sour bile crept up his throat and Blake fought to force it down. "I believe it. Demotteo is the worst kind of slimeball. He's out for himself. He's a self-centered little prick just like his buddy Shaw. They make a good match —lawyer and client. It's all about control, money, and greed. In their world, there isn't anything else."

She shook her head. "Killing thousands of people for money. It's sickening."

Blake nodded. "There is some good news. The CDC and the epidemic task force are reporting there haven't been any new cases of the chimera virus in the past eight hours. They believe the worst is over. If there aren't any new cases over the next forty-eight hours the quarantine will be lifted, and people can get back to their lives. Dr.

Pierson said because Cherenkov had genetically altered the smallpox and Marburg to kill quickly most people were dead within a few hours before having the chance to infect others. In a way, it was the downfall of the master plan of killing as many as possible. At least we think that was the goal."

"What's the latest causality count? I'm almost afraid to ask."

"Too many." He heard the bitterness in his voice. "Four thousand and seventy-one."

She wrung her hands in her lap.

"The nuclear preparedness exercise at Nellis air force base is still a go for tomorrow. The officials want to move forward especially after the release of the virus. The more we're prepared now, the better in the future if there is another nuclear plant attack or biological threat like this one.

"I'm beginning to think the monthly exercise was the target all along and the release in the casino was a test to see how well the virus worked. It makes some sense."

"You might be right."

"I'm supposed to be reporting at the exercise about what it feels like wearing a protective suit. It's ironic, considering I've been stuck wearing one a few times in the past few days. I can't wait to go home and take a long hot shower."

"I'll be joining you. I'm glad to be out of the damn thing. I can't imagine wearing one all the time. We're going to have to do it one more time. Chambers is suggesting that everyone at the exercise wears protective gear especially with Diaz and Morozov on the loose. We don't know if they took some of the virus with them. We'll come up with a plan first thing in the morning for everyone's safety. Mike's been running back and forth dealing with our business at SecuraCorp, and at the FBI. Thank goodness, our new temporary secretary is experienced and knows what to do without much guidance when we're absent otherwise we wouldn't have a business at all at this point. I will be glad to have Michelle back. Don't tell her. I miss having her around."

"I'm sure she'll be happy to get back work."

"Mike and a couple agents are trying to discover why Shaw did all this. The bastard has a motive for everything he does. This time I'm baffled."

"So am I. It feels personal even though what he's done hasn't been targeted at us, at least not yet."

"Let's hope there isn't more to come and what we've witnessed is the end of Shaw's plan. The fallout has been bad enough. It could have been worse. We could have had a pandemic on our hands." He paused before speaking again. "In any case, the DA's office and the FBI are working around the clock collecting and analyzing evidence so we can finally arrest the bastard." He grabbed her hand. "Then it will be over."

She nudged him with her elbow. "Can we go home now?"

A news chopper thundered overhead, dipped, and zoomed off in the opposite direction.

In the distance, he spotted the local and state cops guarding the perimeter of the facility holding back a flood or reporters. "It looks like the locals and the CDC's team have everything under control." He wrapped his arm around her shoulder and whispered in her ear. "Now I'm really looking forward to that long hot shower with you."

CHAPTER FOURTEEN

At the Bean and Waffle House on Camino Al Norte in North Las Vegas, Whitney popped the last bite of the egg, cheese and avocado breakfast sandwich in her mouth and looked out the window. At 11:30 a.m., the sun gleamed in the cloudless blue sky promising beautiful weather. The morning's death count had remained the same as last night's; four thousand and seventy-one. Not a single person who had been infected had survived. Even though so many people had died, it was good news. No new cases meant no new infections and the chance of infecting others. Life was slowly returning to normal, as normal as it could be under the circumstances.

She'd checked in with her boss first thing to update him on the events at ShawBioGen. Travis was happy they'd found the lab and hoped the worst was over with the chimera virus. She had called Sofia and Angel. Both were happy and busy adjusting to their new locations. Whitney clutched her cup of tea with both hands and took a sip. She hoped the girls would be able to come home in a few days.

They would never have discovered the lab if it hadn't

been for the person behind the emails. Whoever sent them probably had saved a lot more lives. For that, she was grateful. Whitney wanted that person to be her father, a deep aching want, cutting into her heart and wouldn't go away. She opened her purse, found her cell phone, and set it on the table. Her fingers quivered over the keypad. She typed in a message.

We found the lab

She hit the 'send' button. Whitney didn't want to do it, but she had to know. She keyed in another message and hesitated then finally found the courage to sent it.

If you're my father, prove it

Her breath hitched in her throat and her body shuddered from the inside out, the anticipation consuming. She stared at the screen and waited. Seconds went by and ten minutes later, no reply. Disappointed, she chucked the phone back in her purse. What was she doing? It was stupid to think she'd get a reply—because it wasn't her father, simply someone who clearly wanted to help. But who? Who else knew about Nathan's plan? Whitney drank the rest of her tea and was about to get up and leave when Hal and Angela walked through the restaurant door.

Hal slid into the booth across from her. "Blake wanted us to meet him here. He's on his way."

"How are you doing?" Angela asked as she slipped into the seat beside Hal.

"I'm really wiped out this morning. I think we all ended up dehydrated being in those suits for so long."

A young waitress with long, blond curly hair stopped at the table and shot Hal a big smile. "What can I get you."

"Just a coffee."

Angela glanced up at the woman. "The same."

"Did you want more tea?" the waitress asked, her eyes slowly drifting away from Hal.

Whitney noticed the way the woman was making googly eyes at him. She stopped herself from laughing out loud. "Please. And a coffee."

As Blake walked through the restaurant door, the waitress returned with their drinks.

He tossed his keys on the table and slid in next to Whitney. He kissed her on the cheek. "Forensics uncovered two million dollars deposited ten days ago, in an off-shore bank account in St. Lucia in one Demotteo's kid's names."

Whitney looked at him. "At least they found a trail."

"Except he lawyered-up as soon as I told him what we found."

Angela shook her head. "That's pretty messed up. A lawyer asking for a lawyer."

"It still doesn't link him to Shaw, does it? I can't wait to get my hands on that asshole."

"Not yet. The guys are still digging."

Hal opened a cream container and dumped it in his coffee. "What about Dr. Death?"

"Cherenkov lawyered-up too. Chambers said the guy hasn't said a word since he was arrested. He'll change his tune as soon as Jason Kurtz tells him they're going for the death penalty. They all talk when the death penalty is on the table."

"Nathan never did," Whitney said.

Blake took a drink of his coffee. "Shaw is different. He'd never admit to anything even with a gun pointed at his head or if he were being tortured. An admission of guilt would mean he failed. Failing doesn't go over well when you're a control-freak psychopath."

"We have to find evidence to connect Nathan to the virus attack." Her muscles turned taut and anxiety betrayed in her voice. "Otherwise he's going to get away with it. He can't." Her emotions had already been stretched to the limit the moment Jerry had been killed. She couldn't take another hit.

Blake grasped her hand. "He won't."

"Nope, he won't," Hal said. "There are four people at this table who will make damn sure he doesn't."

"No way," Angela said. "He will get what's coming to him."

"We'll find the connection whether it's a money trail or something else and nail him." Blake squeezed her hand. "Everyone is working really hard. They want this as much as we do...Chambers...Kurtz."

"What's the plan at the nuclear preparedness exercise?" Hal glanced at his chunky silver watch. "We have to be there in about forty-five minutes."

"Chambers doesn't believe Diaz or Morozov have any of the virus but to be safe he spoke to the organizers and it was agreed participants should be in protective gear. A massive shipment of biosafety suits arrived at the base early this morning. Unless Cherenkov or Demotteo start talking and we know what's going on for sure, that's the plan."

Hal shook his head. "Great. Two hours in the baking sun wearing a rubber suit."

"Big-time fun," Angela added.

"I agree. I thought we were done with those damn things. They'll have a biocontainment-type cooling station set up inside one of the hangars to make sure everyone stays hydrated." His cell phone rang. He retrieved the phone from his shirt pocket and answered it. "Yeah—okay—I'll head out now." He rammed the phone in back in his pocket.

"That was Chambers. Apparently, Demotteo wants to talk to me. Only me."

Whitney straightened in the seat. "That's a positive sign."

"It sure is," Hal said, then gulped down rest of his drink and set the cup on the table. "We should get going." He glanced at Angela. "We know how the organizers don't like late-comers."

Angela laughed and slapped Hal in the arm. "Give me a break. I was stuck in traffic the last time."

Blake downed what was left of his coffee, snatched up his keys and dropped a twenty-dollar bill on the table. He eased out of the booth and stood.

Whitney got up and swung the strap of her purse over her shoulder.

"Stay with Hal and Angela and follow them to the air force base. I'll meet you guys there." He pushed the door open.

When they walked outside there was a deathlike stillness in the air. Traffic zoomed by. Her skin prickled and the tiny hairs on the back of her neck stood at attention. Whitney had the weirdest feeling someone was watching her.

❊ ❊ ❊

Inside the FBI interrogation room, Blake leaned against the wall with his arms crossed over his chest. Demotteo sat at the table with his hands cuffed in front of him. Chambers and the DA were on the other side of the tinted two-way glass listening.

"I'm here. Start talking."

Lines dug across Demotteo's forehead. He cleared his throat. "First you need to guarantee my family will be picked up immediately and moved to a safe location that I choose."

His body stiffened. The guy was already pissing him off. "You don't get to dictate and negotiate terms after what you've done. Tell me what you know, and I assure you the FBI will do everything they can to make sure your family is out of harm's way."

Demotteo paused for a moment. His eyes drifted to the ceiling and then to the floor. "I need that assurance. It's the only thing I'm asking for."

Blake glanced at the two-way glass already knowing Chambers' answer. "Fine. You have my assurance. Now get to the God damn point."

"Dr. Dimitri Cherenkov designed and produced the chimera virus."

"Old news."

"When he crafted the chimera virus, he named it Resurrect. He's a very dangerous man."

Resurrect. The sick assholes named the virus. Blake rammed his hands into his jeans pockets to stop himself from beating the crap out of the guy. "And you're not dangerous?"

The metal cuffs jangled along with the heavy gold chains around Demotteo's neck when he shifted in the chair. "I was just doing what I was supposed to do."

"Under Nathan Shaw's orders. The smallpox sample was taken from a lab in Texas by James Nova and the Marburg was from Matthew Fielding. We already know that. More old news. How much of the virus was used in the attack at the Four Spades?"

"Very little. Perhaps enough to fill a small vial."

"Enough to kill almost five thousand people." Blake wanted to ring the guy's stubby neck.

"After Dimitri created the virus and produced the plastic-coated particles, he made extra and gave it to Eduardo."

When they'd searched the lab they'd only found a small amount of the virus enough to confirm the biological agent was on-site.

"How much extra did Cherenkov produce?"

Demotteo huffed and puffed and nervously rubbed his thumbs together. "Five kilos."

Blake's jaw dropped open. Five kilos? Enough to kill tens of thousands of people. He hammered his fist down on the table. "Where are Diaz and Morozov?"

"I don't know where Cherenkov's assistant went. He could be anywhere."

No more games. Blake gripped the edge of the small metal table and heaved it across the room into the wall below the two-way mirror. He gritted his teeth. "Where is Diaz? What is he planning to do?" Blake snatched the man by his neck and extracted him out of the chair. He forced him against the wall and held him there leaving his feet dangling a few inches off the floor.

"Okay. Okay. He has five drones armed with the chimera—."

"Shit!" Blake released Demotteo's neck, dropping him. He ran out of the room and raced into the connecting room where Chambers and the DA were waiting.

"Get a chopper in the air and search an eight to ten-mile radius around Nellis Airforce Base. Make sure all the employees here get into disposable suits. Then alert the media and get an emergency broadcast sent out warning people to stay inside and prepare for another possible biological attack."

* * *

Five miles south of Nellis Air Force Base, Eduardo crouched behind a massive boulder dressed in a protective suit and carefully attached the small wire basket to the bottom of the last drone. A jet rumbled high in the sky and rocketed by, the sonic boom roaring seconds behind it.

After he secured the basket, he pulled on a pair of rubber gloves and inserted the glass jar containing the virus and attached the microchip timer and blasting cap. The sun beat at the back of his neck. Perspiration dripped down his spine under his T-shirt. He stood and set the drone down with both hands cautiously on the ground beside the four others. Next to the drones sat his full-face respirator, a military-grade radar jammer and the Russian-made RPG-7 he'd bought on the black market through his one of his many drug connections in the country.

Earlier, he had driven past the reporter, spotted her and the others on the sidewalk outside a restaurant. He wondered if she'd noticed him. It didn't matter.

Viktor didn't want to come along for the ride to help him prepare. Eduardo showed him how things were handled back in his country when you weren't willing to pull your own weight. He had hog-tied the man and shot him in the back of the head, his body broiling in the trunk of the car he'd stolen. He had replaced the van he had at the lab in case the authorities were searching for it. The first thing Eduardo had learned from Pablo Sanchez when he'd worked for him at the cartel's compound in Bogota was leave no witnesses.

He walked to the car parked between the boulder and a soaring cactus, reached inside the open window and grabbed a bottle of water from the passenger seat. After removing the cap, he gulped down all the liquid and dropped the bottle on the ground. Eduardo checked his wristwatch. It was twelve-thirty, a half hour to go. He knew he wouldn't be returning home to Colombia. The best he could do now was to make sure the plan was executed.

❈ ❈ ❈

Thirteen miles northeast of downtown Las Vegas, Whitney stood inside a hangar at Nellis Air Force Base waiting for her new cameraman, Kyle Barker to arrive. She'd worked with him in the past, but it wasn't the same. She was sad Jerry wasn't with her. He should've have been. Melancholy surged through her and she peered outside.

A strong south wind blew against her face. The base was situated on 11,300 acres. Two runways stretched parallel to the east across the base. Most of the facilities were located west of the runways. To the east was the live ordinance loading area, control tower and bomber pad. The base's golf course was on the southern edge while MH-60 search and rescue helicopters worked from the Jolly Pad in the far northwest corner.

In the distance, most of the hundreds of volunteers, military, first responders, police, firefighters, and medical personnel were dressed in protective suits. Behind them, a long line of emergency vehicles flanked the horizon. The turnout for the exercise was huge. More than the organizers had anticipated. Whitney believed it was because of the chimera virus attack. People wanted to help, and at the same time learn how to protect themselves and their families in the future if there was another attack at a nuclear facility or biological threat.

While Hal and Angela were busy chatting with two FBI agents, Whitney walked to the changing area located behind the large cooling station, took a seat on one of the wooden benches provided and began putting on her biosafety suit. Hal and Angela had already changed into their gear except for their respirator masks. She taped the legs of her jeans tight around her ankles with duct tape then stood and put on the suit. She still had twenty minutes before she was supposed to go on the air. Before zipping up the suit, Whitney pulled her cell phone from her back pocket and checked her messages. There was one new one. It was the reply to her email asking the sender to prove he was her father. She tapped the 'open' icon. Her heart skipped a beat.

Whale watching at Otters Rock

The air vacuumed out of her lungs and she gasped. *It can't be.* Whitney read the reply over and over trying to understand how it was possible. It wasn't. Her skin tingled and instincts prickled. No one knew she and her father had gone whale watching at Otters Rock in Oregon where she had grown up. It was after her mother had died when Whitney was a teenager. No one. It was one of the many secret trips they'd taken together each time her father had returned from an assignment in a foreign country. The trips were important to her father and to her. He wanted to make sure she enjoyed each one before he left the country again, sometimes for months, hunting down the next story. She was too confused to send a reply, couldn't even think straight.

A hand clamped down on her shoulder.

She spun.

"Didn't mean to scare you."

Narrow blue eyes stared back at her.

It was Kyle, her cameraman. He had a thin face with a chiseled chin and hair the color of stainless steel. He'd been working at News3 for over a decade.

She exhaled a long breath, shut off the phone, and slid it back into her pocket. She needed to focus if she was going to get through the live report. "That's okay. I'm still a little jumpy after the virus attack." She lied. She had to because what she had just read on her phone was like something out of the Twilight Zone. Impossible. Whitney had to admit she was spooked.

"It took longer than expected to get through security. The satellite van is parked on the runway ready to broadcast."

"You'd better get changed. We don't have much time. The suits and masks are over there." Whitney pointed to two wooden skids stacked high with cardboard boxes containing the protective outfits. She quickly did up her suit and pulled over the adhesive flap to cover the zipper, and then put on rubber gloves, securing them around her wrists with tape.

Once Kyle was ready, Hal and Angela walked with them out of the hangar to the exercise staging area in the middle of the second runway with their respirator masks tucked under their arms. She couldn't focus, her mind darting in every direction. Her emotions had already been stretched to the limit after Jerry had been killed. She couldn't take another emotional hit especially someone pretending to be her father. How could anyone else know about Otters Rock? Whitney wished she had the answer.

Behind them, boots thumped against the pavement. Groups of stern-faced military personal strutted by chatting in regular army fatigues not concerned everyone else on the runway had biosafety suits on. Hal and Angela headed to where the officials were gathered.

In front of the satellite van, Whitney shifted from foot to foot, clutching the microphone mentally preparing herself to go on the air. A yard away, Kyle hiked the camera up on his shoulder and raised his gloved fingers in the air ready to begin the countdown.

Suddenly air raid sirens blared.

The loud two-tone sound wailed, the eerie ghostly sound reverberating deep in her bones.

She lowered the mic and scanned the area.

"Is that supposed to be happening?" Kyle shouted.

Whitney shook her head. "I have no idea." She noticed most of the participants had stopped what they were doing and appeared confused. Out of the corner of her eye, she spotted Hal and Angela charging toward her. Angela was waving her arms in the air.

As they approached, Hal's voice bellowed over the howling siren. "It's not part of the exercise. There's a possible biological attack coming."

Not again. Whitney's eyes drifted to the clusters of military personnel not wearing protective suits. There were hundreds on the runway and it didn't include the more than forty thousand military staff and families on the base.

She swallowed a curse and took off running. "Everyone get in the hangar!"

＊ ＊ ＊

Blake's heart pounded as he sped the truck down the interstate toward Nellis Air Force Base. Nothing like wearing a full biosafety suit while driving. Drivers raced by in the opposite lane craning their necks and did a double-take. He unrolled his window and turned up the radio. The male radio announcer's baritone voice rumbled, heralding the broadcast of a possible biological attack. Seconds later the electronic robotic voice of the state emergency broadcast system grated through the truck's speakers. Now he knew why Demotteo was adamant about moving his family. He knew another attack was imminent.

Blake needed to find Diaz before he sent up the drones. The fallout from five kilos of the chimera virus would be epically devastating and ultimately create a pandemic. He had called Whitney and his message had gone to her voicemail. He's also tried Hal and Angela with no success. He prayed they were in their protective suits.

He felt helpless. At the moment, there was nothing more he could do for the residents of Las Vegas. Blake hoped people were taking the warning seriously. His hands tightened around the steering wheel. He had to find Diaz before it was too late.

To the east, an FBI helicopter circled, its blades chopping through the low translucent clouds.

His cell phone rang.

He snatched up the phone from the dash and pressed put it on speaker. "Yeah."

"I've got a visual on a car and one person in the middle of nowhere on the east side of O'Bannon Road about five miles south of the perimeter of the air base."

Adrenaline shot through his veins. It had to be Diaz.

"One sec." Blake steered onto the shoulder and threw the vehicle in park. He popped open the glove box and grabbed a pen and a napkin.

"Give me the coordinates."

The pilot rattled them off.

He jotted them down and tossed the pen on the passenger seat. "Got it. Keep your eyes on him. Thanks, man."

"Roger that."

Blake keyed the location into the GPS and hurled the truck into drive. As he floored the gas pedal, he watched the helicopter dip and re-circle the area of Diaz's position.

A thunderous bang jolted him in the seat.

The helicopter's cockpit burst into an orange and red fireball. His heart stopped and sweat rolled down his face. "Shit!"

Thick black smoke billowed out of the fuselage. Debris arched and rained down like stones. The chopper's engine whined and screeched, and then the helicopter cartwheeled toward the ground. Seconds later, he heard another explosion and saw plumes of gray smoke curling high on the horizon.

Diaz did this. Blake hammered his gloved palm down on the steering wheel. "God damn it." He had to have taken down the chopper with an RPG. He snatched his cell phone and called 911.

Afterward, he shook his head. He knew the pilot. Jason Rourke. He'd worked with him for ten years when he was still with the Bureau. The guy had kids, grandkids.

As he got closer to Diaz's location, his eyes shifted from the road to the GPS. Within a sixteenth of a mile of the coordinates, Blake rolled to a stop under a tall yucca tree. He reached under the seat and pulled out his Glock. Ejecting the magazine and double-checking that it was full he quickly jammed it upward with his palm back in place. He fished out an extra full magazine from the glove box then realized the protective suit didn't have pockets. He chucked the magazine aside on the seat and glanced at the GPS.

Diaz wasn't far, about three hundred yards to the west.

Blake got out of the truck and cautiously walked in that direction with his gun raised. He eyed a large black drone in the air hovering. It pitched right and traveled north. Blake sprinted the best he could in the awkward suit and stopped behind a large boulder. He flattened his back against the rock and inched his way to the other side.

Diaz was wearing a blue biosafety suit and was clutching a large silver remote control with both hands. His head was tilted toward the sky.

He stepped out from behind the boulder and kept his gun trained on the man. Next to Diaz was an RPG, three rockets, and four multi-copter drones on the ground with containers, blasting caps, and timers attached. Blake squeezed the trigger.

The shot drove into Diaz's leg just below the knee. He dropped the remote control on the corner of a jagged rock and fell to the ground on his ass. The case smashed into pieces jamming the stick controls.

The drone was still hovering.

Blake lowered his weapon and dove for the remote control knowing the UAV had a microchip timer. He didn't know when the device was set to go off.

As he slid to the ground on his stomach, Diaz snatched the shoulder of the rubber suit and punched him repeatedly in the side of the mask. He wound his arms around Blake's wrists making it impossible for him to use his weapon. Diaz was suddenly on top of him, staring at him with clenched teeth. They rolled back and forth at least a half dozen times, dirt spitting up around them. Blake felt the man's fingers clawing, trying to remove his respirator mask. Finally, Blake was able to wrestle his arms free.

A gunshot cracked.

Birds in a nearby tree dispersed, wings flapping in every direction.

The bullet blasted into the right side of Diaz's chest and into his heart.

Blood spewed and splatted against the clear visor of Blake's mask. He heaved the man's body off of him. For a few seconds, he lay on his back, gasping. *The drone!* He jumped to his feet, picked up the remote control and tried steering the UAV back to him so he could get it on the ground, but the transmitter wasn't responding, the controls stuck leaving the drone hovering in the same spot.

He had to take it down. There was no margin for error.

His eyes whipped to the rocket launcher. He scooped the weapon off the ground, loaded a rocket into the muzzle, locked the breech and perched the unit on his shoulder. The heat from the explosive warhead would disintegrate the virus. It had to.

Staring through the viewfinder he lined up the shot, took a deep breath, exhaled, and pressed the hammer trigger.

The warhead popped and swooshed hitting the underside of the drone. The UAV exploded with a flash followed by a small fireball, destroying the unit and annihilating the virus.

Back at his truck, Blake picked up his cell phone from the dash, put it on speaker, and called Chambers. He'd be stuck wearing the biosafety suit until the scene was cleared by the CDC's Rapid Response Team.

"Chambers."

"Diaz is dead. I need a biocontainment team immediately dispatched to my location." He let out a long weary breath. "It's over."

CHAPTER FIFTEEN

At five-thirty Whitney walked to the other side of the hangar and peered outside. Twilight had transcended over the air force base. Streaks of turquoise and indigo painted the sky, the quarter moon a white glowing distant speck high above the bright lights of the base's facilities.

Hal had received word through one of the exercise officials that Blake had gone after Eduardo. Her nerve endings flickered with worry and anxiety, her heart beating a faster than normal. She'd been pacing for hours, waiting, wondering, unable to sit still until she had confirmation he was okay.

"Blake will be fine," Hal said and placed his hand on her shoulder. "I'm sure he'll be here soon."

Angela touched the arm of her suit. "I'm sure he's okay too."

She could feel how sticky her skin felt under her clothes inside the suit and the stress of waiting for Blake wasn't helping.

Whitney looked around. She was sure everyone was sick and tired of being wrapped in rubber. Kyle was busy filming the scene and chatting with some of the officials. The military men and women who weren't in protective suits earlier had quick-changed into them the second they'd learned another virus attack could happen. Until officials received word they were safe they'd ordered participants to remain in their gear.

Whitney turned. She saw Blake strutting into the hangar dressed in jeans with his white shirt rolled up to his forearms. He smiled when he saw her. Her breath caught in her throat. He wouldn't be in his regular clothes if there was still a threat.

Whitney tugged off the mask and dropped it on the ground. She ran to him and threw her arms around him. The love she witnessed in the depth of his eyes warmed her and made her grateful he was in her life. "I was so worried about you."

He held her tight and kissed her, long and eager. "I was worried about you too."

Hal took off his mask and patted him on the back. He shot Blake a big crooked grin. "Welcome back, man."

"I'm glad to see everyone is safe."

"I told you he'd was okay." Angela removed her respirator mask. "Good to see you."

He gave Angela a nod and a smile. "Can you let the officials know there is no longer a threat? We're all clear. They can verify it with Chambers and the CDC."

"Sure," Angela said

"What happened?" Hal asked, as he twisted his head and watched Angela walk away.

"Diaz is dead. I was able to save the remaining kilos of the virus before they were released."

Hal ran his fingers through his hair. "Kilos?"

Whitney's eyes widened. She couldn't believe Nathan had produced kilos of the chimera virus. If he had succeeded with his plan, the whole city could have been affected. "He planned on taking out half of Las Vegas."

"It looks that way. Shaw paid Cherenkov to make five kilos of the virus. Diaz had the virus in glass containers attached to five UAVs with blasting caps and timers. They could have exploded at any time. When I got there Diaz already had one drone in the air. I took it down with an RPG rocket, frying the virus but not before he shot down an FBI helicopter." He looked at Hal and his expression turned somber. "Jason Roarke was piloting."

Hal shook his head. "Did he make it?"

Blake hesitated, and Whitney knew the answer.

"No."

Another body to add to the thousands dead because of Nathan. Why? Anger gripped her, and she had a difficult keeping it at bay.

Blake wrapped his arm around her shoulder. "It's over."

It wasn't over, not in Whitney's mind.

＊ ＊ ＊

In the coffee shop on Flamingo Road, Whitney sat across from Hal sipping a cup of tea. Cinnamon and icing sugar filled the air and made her stomach growl. The shop was empty except for an older woman with pale blonde hair working behind the counter and a male baker adding a tray of freshly baked donuts inside the glass display cabinet.

"How's Blake?"

"He's okay, exhausted. He fell asleep a half hour after we got home. It's been a long few days. Thanks for meeting me."

"Anytime. You know that. Guess you couldn't sleep."

Whitney cupped her mug with both hands and stared at her tea. "Guess you couldn't either."

"I have a feeling you're here because you have some unfinished business."

He'd read right through her. Whitney wasn't surprised. "It's not over for me. Nathan has taken so much from us. I want to know why."

"I don't blame you. You guys have gone through hell because of that asshole."

They had, and if she didn't do something about it, it would never end. There was a beat of awkward silence between them.

"What do you want to do?"

She blew out a breath and thought for a moment. "I'm not exactly sure. I want to speak to him first. I need to know why he killed all those people and Jerry."

"And after that?"

Whitney was sure Hal knew what she wanted. She wanted Nathan dead but couldn't bring herself to say the words out loud. She pushed aside her cup of tea, angry she was even thinking this way. "I don't know, Hal. I just don't know."

As if sensing her turmoil, he patted her hand. "I'll go with you to watch your back. Afterward, it's up to you. I'm good either way."

❊ ❊ ❊

At the bottom of the hill leading to Nathan's house, Whitney sat in the driver's seat of Hal's car with the engine running.

"You sure about this?"

This was the only way. "Yes."

"Give me ten minutes to get in position." Hal got out of the car and shut the door.

She glanced in the side mirror and watched him remove a long black duffel bag from the trunk containing his sniper rifle. Then the trunk closed.

He popped his head inside the window. "I'll have my eyes on you at all times. You'll be safe."

She nodded, and her stomach knotted as he sprinted across the road and into the darkness.

Hal had taken her to the spot where he would be located behind Nathan's house overlooking the golf course. He'd also showed her the easiest way to get there without causing any suspicion. Her eyes drifted to the digital clock on the dash. The red lights glared back. It was ten-fifteen and she was sure Nathan would be awake. Her heart pounded. She knew deep down she was doing the right thing.

Ten minutes snailed by and felt like an hour. Whitney put the car into drive and crept up the hill. She steered into Nathan's driveway and shut off the engine.

The outside of the house was lit up. Flood lights beamed and cast eerie shadows around the massive home and property. Her insides shook. Whitney inhaled then exhaled a long breath trying to settle her nerves. She opened her purse for the third time and made sure her gun was inside. After getting out of the car, she walked to the door and rang the doorbell.

The door opened a crack and different butler's face appeared. This one was much younger.

"I need to speak with Nathan."

"Please come in. He's been expecting you."

Expecting her? A deep primal fear dug deep to her bones. For a second Whitney wanted to bolt but if she didn't do this Nathan would never be out of their lives. She walked into the foyer and followed the butler to the living room, her gaze roaming, checking her surroundings for possible danger.

The house smelled of earth, sweet spice, and burnt cedar wood. Nathan was sitting in a high-back chair with his legs crossed reading a book. He was dressed in a powder blue tracksuit. A cigar sat in an ashtray beside him. He closed the book and set it on his lap.

"Miss Steel. What do I owe the pleasure of your visit at this time of night?"

Whitney clung to her shoulder bag knowing the Ruger LC9 was only a heartbeat away if she needed it.

"You know why I'm here. Why did you have Jerry killed and thousands of other innocent people?"

He held out his hand and gestured to the chair next to him. "Have a seat."

"No. I'll stand."

"Suit yourself. Do you believe I would be stupid enough to implicate myself in such a horrible deed?"

No, she didn't. "But you were expecting me. You must have something to say."

"Smart woman. I've always liked that about you."

She was already tired of Nathan's typical cat-and-mouse game, never letting his guard down while talking in circles.

Whitney wasn't going to allow him to have the upper hand. "We have evidence that you are the one who ordered and footed the bill for the virus attack at the Four Spades and the failed attack at Nellis Air Force Base. Eduardo is dead. Dr. Cherenkov, Dell Summers, and your lawyer have been arrested. They all like to chat a lot especially when their lives are on the line."

"Then why haven't the authorities arrested me?" He looked around the room. "Where is your dear husband?"

She wasn't discussing Blake. This was about her, what

she wanted. Answers. "Why did you do it, Nathan? Isn't it enough that you have spent years working to destroy my world?"

"That's a little melodramatic, don't you think?"

She thought about all the people he'd killed even before the virus attack. Mason, Claire, Kate, George...

Anger bubbled up inside her. She hugged her purse tighter trying to stop herself from pulling out the gun and shooting him.

"My new lawyer says I haven't been thinking properly, cognitive issues, and perhaps lately I have made some poor choices due to my medical condition."

Whitney laughed. "Poor choices? Give me a break. Killing almost five thousand people and that's the best you can come up with. It's pretty lame even for you to use a medical condition to justify murdering people. Do you really think I'm that stupid?"

"Miss Steel. I never said I did anything. I'm just letting you know I haven't been well." He took a puff of his cigar and plumes of smoke curled around his head. "I have an inoperable brain tumor. Glioblastoma multiforme. It has impaired my judgment in many areas of my life due to the position of the large mass and the damage to the vital neurological pathways. The tumor has invaded and compressed my brain tissue. If I am arrested, and that is a big if, my lawyer will ensure I don't go to prison again. I can assure you he's done his homework."

He could get away with mass murder. Bile crept up her throat and she choked it down. "I don't believe you."

Nathan smirked. "I'd be more than happy to release my medical records if needed. At this point, they aren't needed because I haven't done anything wrong."

Anger sizzled. Whitney seized the strap of her purse

with both hands. "If that's all you have to say then I'm leaving." She turned and walked to the door, her feet pounding on the expensive marble floor.

"Have a good night, Miss Steel."

She slammed the door on the way out.

Nathan was using a brain tumor as an excuse for killing kids, families. She got into the car, rammed the transmission into reverse and barreled out of the driveway.

Whitney sped down the hill and continued driving a half block west. She parked the car in the corner of the golf club's parking lot away from any lampposts. After shutting off the engine, she popped the trunk and go out. Heaving her purse inside, she closed the trunk. A light breeze flowed through her hair and cooled her skin but did nothing to simmer her anger. She didn't believe Nathan's brain tumor story. He'd probably paid off his doctors and was using someone else's medical test results. Anything to get away with murder. Not this time.

She sprinted through the golf course keeping to the outer edge away from any light. Five minutes later, she stopped to catch her breath and peered up at the steep jagged rocks. She grasped the first rock and maneuvered her feet and hands up each one careful not to slip. When she reached the top, Whitney bent down with her hands on her knees and forced her breathing to an even pace.

A few yards away, Hal was on his stomach between two large rocks with a CheyTac M200.408 sniper rifle pointed at Nathan's living room window.

He looked up at her and she knew he understood exactly what she wanted, what she needed to do.

They would never be free of the Nathan. It was the only way.

Hal lumbered to his feet and brushed his hands off on

his pants. "You know. I can do this so you don't have to. I already told Blake I had no problem looking after Shaw."

Whitney told herself over and over there was no other choice. Nathan would never take responsibility for what he'd done and next time it could be her or Blake or one of the girls. He'd never stop coming after them. Whitney couldn't live with herself if something happened to them. "No. I'll do it." She swallowed the rock-like lump in her throat and lowered to her stomach.

It was the only way.

Aligning the scope, she aimed the crosshairs on the back of Nathan's head. She inhaled a long steady breath expelling the air even slower to stop her hands from shaking. After chambering a round Whitney pushed the bolt forward and closed it. She placed her finger on the trigger guard and sucked in one last deep breath, let two-thirds out, and held it.

She squeezed the trigger gently and exhaled.

Nathan's head jerked violently forward then backward, the bullet driving through his brain. Death was instant. His body slumped over the arm of the chair.

Tears blurred her vision and rolled down her face. Whitney looked away, her body shaking as years of heartache, loss, and fear let loose.

It was finally over.

CHAPTER SIXTEEN

Palm Beach, Aruba - Two days later...

A fifty-foot yacht rocked in the distance like a cradle as waves cascaded over the shore, the lapping water soothing Whitney's nerves. Squabbling seabirds circled and dove, plucking their evening dinner from the turquoise water. Blake walked beside her holding her hand. She was positive he knew she'd killed Nathan. He had mentioned whoever had delivered the shot had done the right thing. The man needed to be stopped. Four thousand and ninety-four people had died from the Resurrect virus and the country was quickly coming to grips that a biological threat could happen again if lab samples ever ended up in the wrong hands. Security was being beefed up at all labs in the state as well as throughout the country.

Before they'd caught their flight to Aruba, the director of the CDC issued a statement explaining why the agency hadn't alerted the public when Matthew Fielding and the two men at the warehouse had become infected, saying they believed it was an isolated incident because Matthew Fielding had worked at a BSL-4 lab and had probably infected himself.

Angel ran along the beach in white shorts and T-shirt,

232 | KIM CRESSWELL

sand and water spraying behind her bare feet. Blake's parents walked briskly behind her trying to catch up with the bundle of energy.

"You're here!" She leapt into Whitney's arms and smacked a kiss on her forehead.

Whitney hugged her. "I'm so happy to see you. I've missed you so much."

"Missed you." She cocked her head to one side and pointed to Hal, Angela and Mike chatting with Sofia. "Why are they here?"

"Everyone really needed a vacation. Is that okay?"

Angel nodded, and her eyes shone. "Can we have a party?"

Blake grinned. "We sure can after supper." Angel scurried out of Whitney's arms and into his. She rested her head on his shoulder, her small hands gripping the sides of his neck.

The sight warmed Whitney's heart.

Angel suddenly wiggled out of his arms to the ground and raced toward Sofia. When she got to her, she clung to the young woman's leg.

"Glad everyone returned in one piece, son. Thank God we don't have to worry about that monster anymore."

"Me too, Dad." Blake gave his mom a hug then looked at Whitney. "Shaw or his pals won't be bothering us ever again."

"It's time to celebrate," Blake's mom said. "Frank, how about we go and get the barbecue started. I made a ton of salads. By the looks of it, we have a hungry crew to feed."

Apparently, Joe Cally and Paul McBride were back at the villa. Whitney was starving. The first time in days.

After Blake's parents walked away, Blake gripped her hand tighter and they strolled along the beach alone.

The evening sky was washed in a pale shade of tangerine orange. Salty hot air blew through her hair and left a tangy taste on the tip of her tongue. They hadn't talked much about what had happened because they were either too exhausted or needed time to process what Nathan had done.

"Do you believe Nathan really had a brain tumor?"

"I doubt it. I think you're right. He bought someone else's test results. It's exactly what he would do. We'll know for sure in a couple days once the autopsy is done."

Regardless if he had a tumor or not, Whitney knew deep down she had made the right choice. She'd never felt this calm and safe in years. It felt good not having to worry or always be looking over her shoulder. She could tell Blake was at peace too by his relaxed features.

"Chambers said Demotteo, Summers, and Dr. Cherenkov are all squawking like parrots vying for the best deal they can get from the DA's office."

"They all deserve the death sentence and nothing less."

"Jason will make sure he gets the death sentence for Demotteo and Cherenkov. He's not interested in any deals. As far as Dell Summers is concerned, he'll probably spend five to ten years behind bars for his part if the judge takes into consideration the threats made against his family. Just because he felt he didn't have a choice, doesn't make it right. He should have contacted the authorities. If he had not as many people would have died."

Part of her felt sorry for Dell Summers. All he had wanted to do was to protect his family. He had to make a tough choice and unfortunately a lot of people had paid the price.

"Who killed the scientist in Texas?"

"Eduardo killed James Nova right after he got his hands on the sample of smallpox. From what we can piece together, Diaz did it for the money and revenge. He'd lost his hefty income source after Pablo Sanchez was killed. Nathan Shaw had dropped the perfect opportunity in his lap. He couldn't say no."

"Did Eduardo kill Matthew Fielding too?"

Blake shook his head. "Shaw's slimeball lawyer finally admitted to killing him. He figured if he took responsibility the death sentence would be taken off the table. He was wrong. The only reason Demotteo was involved in Shaw's scheme was for the huge payout. Pure greed."

"It's always about greed or revenge, isn't it?"

"Always."

It was bothering her that he hadn't asked her about Nathan. "Don't you want to know who killed Nathan?"

Blake put his arm around her shoulder. "I already spoke with Hal. He said he took Shaw out. The bastard is gone. All that matters is he is out of lives for good."

Whitney wasn't surprised Hal had covered for her. She hoped there was no way to trace anything back to him or to her.

An image of her father formed in her mind. The sender of the emails hadn't sent any more messages leaving her with an unfinished feeling. She needed to know who was behind them. Whitney would find out. For now, she had everything she needed right here in paradise for five more days. The man she loved, the girls she loved, good friends, family, and the satisfaction of knowing Nathan Shaw was dead.

They could finally get on with their lives.

AUTHOR'S NOTE

I hope you enjoyed reading *Resurrect* as much as I enjoyed writing the story. Please don't forget to leave a review.

Great news for fans! Watch for *Redemption* (A Whitney Steel Novel - Book Four) coming soon!

If you have enjoyed reading the Whitney Steel romantic thriller series, then you're going to love *Deadly Shadow* (The Assassin Chronicles), the first book in the exciting paranormal thriller series featuring FBI Agent Victory McClane and government assassin Derrick Lynn!

A special thanks to Betty McEachern.

To my fans, readers and reviewers—thank you for your continuing support!

You rock!